The Zeppelin's Passengers

by

E. Phillips Oppenheim

The Zeppelin's Passengers
by E. Phillips Oppenheim

Copyright © 2023

All Rights reserved.
No part of this publication may be reproduced, stored in a retrieval system, or transmitted in any form or by any means, electronic, mechanical, photocopying or Otherwise, without the written permission of the publisher.

The author/editor asserts the moral right to be identified as the author/editor of this work.

ISBN: 978-93-57271-97-4

Published by

DOUBLE 9 BOOKS

2/13-B, Ansari Road
Daryaganj, New Delhi – 110002
info@double9books.com
www.double9books.com
Tel. 011-40042856

This book is under public domain

ABOUT THE AUTHOR

E. Phillips Oppenheim was born on October 22, 1866, in Tohhenham, London, England, to Henrietta Susannah Temperley Budd and Edward John Oppenheim, a leather retailer. After leaving school at age 17, he helped his father in his leather business and used to write in his extra time. His first novel, Expiration (1886), and subsequent thrillers piqued the interest of a wealthy New York businessman who eventually bought out the leather business and made Oppenheim a high-paid director.He is more focused on dedicating most of his time to writing. The novels, volumes of short stories, and plays that followed, numbering more than 150, were about humans with modern heroes, fearless spies, and stylish noblemen. The Long Arm of Mannister (1910), The Moving Finger (1911), and The Great Impersonation (1920) are three of his most famous essays.

CONTENTS

CHAPTER I 7

CHAPTER II 13

CHAPTER III 19

CHAPTER IV 28

CHAPTER V 33

CHAPTER VI 41

CHAPTER VII 46

CHAPTER VIII 54

CHAPTER IX 60

CHAPTER X 66

CHAPTER XI 73

CHAPTER XII 81

CHAPTER XIII 85

CHAPTER XIV 91

CHAPTER XV 97

CHAPTER XVI 102

CHAPTER XVII 107

CHAPTER XVIII 113

CHAPTER XIX 119

CHAPTER XX 125

CHAPTER XXI 131

CHAPTER XXII 136

CHAPTER XXIII 140

CHAPTER XXIV 147

CHAPTER XXV 154

CHAPTER XXVI 162

CHAPTER XXVII 168

CHAPTER XXVIII 175

CHAPTER XXIX 180

CHAPTER XXX 186

CHAPTER XXXI 192

CHAPTER XXXII 197

CHAPTER XXXIII 201

CHAPTER I

"Never heard a sound," the younger of the afternoon callers admitted, getting rid of his empty cup and leaning forward in his low chair. "No more tea, thank you, Miss Fairclough. Done splendidly, thanks. No, I went to bed last night soon after eleven—the Colonel had been route marching us all off our legs—and I never awoke until reveille this morning. Sleep of the just, and all that sort of thing, but a jolly sell, all the same! You hear anything of it, sir?" he asked, turning to his companion, who was seated a few feet away.

Captain Griffiths shook his head. He was a man considerably older than his questioner, with long, nervous face, and thick black hair streaked with grey. His fingers were bony, his complexion, for a soldier, curiously sallow, and notwithstanding his height, which was considerable, he was awkward, at times almost uncouth. His voice was hard and unsympathetic, and his contributions to the tea-table talk had been almost negligible.

"I was up until two o'clock, as it happened," he replied, "but I knew nothing about the matter until it was brought to my notice officially."

Helen Fairclough, who was doing the honours for Lady Cranston, her absent hostess, assumed the slight air of superiority to which the circumstances of the case entitled her.

"I heard it distinctly," she declared; "in fact it woke me up. I hung out of the window, and I could hear the engine just as plainly as though it were over the golf links."

The young subaltern sighed.

"Rotten luck I have with these things," he confided. "That's three times they've been over, and I've neither heard nor seen one. This time they say that it had the narrowest shave on earth of coming down. Of course, you've heard of the observation car found on Dutchman's Common this morning?"

The girl assented.

"Did you see it?" she enquired.

"Not a chance," was the gloomy reply. "It was put on two covered trucks and sent up to London by the first train. Captain Griffiths can tell you what it was like, I dare say. You were down there, weren't you, sir?"

"I superintended its removal," the latter informed them. "It was a very uninteresting affair."

"Any bombs in it?" Helen asked.

"Not a sign of one. Just a hard seat, two sets of field-glasses and a telephone. It seems to have got caught in some trees and been dragged off."

"How exciting!" the girl murmured. "I suppose there wasn't any one in it?"

Griffiths shook his head.

"I believe," he explained, "that these observation cars, although they are attached to most of the Zeppelins, are seldom used in night raids."

"I should like to have seen it, all the same," Helen confessed.

"You would have been disappointed," her informant assured her. "By-the-by," he added, a little awkwardly, "are you not expecting Lady Cranston back this evening?"

"I am expecting her every moment. The car has gone down to the station to meet her."

Captain Griffiths appeared to receive the news with a certain undemonstrative satisfaction. He leaned back in his chair with the air of one who is content to wait.

"Have you heard, Miss Fairclough," his younger companion enquired, a little diffidently, "whether Lady Cranston had any luck in town?"

Helen Fairclough looked away. There was a slight mist before her eyes.

"I had a letter this morning," she replied. "She seems to have heard nothing at all encouraging so far."

"And you haven't heard from Major Felstead himself, I suppose?"

The girl shook her head.

"Not a line," she sighed. "It's two months now since we last had a letter."

"Jolly bad luck to get nipped just as he was doing so well," the young man observed sympathetically.

"It all seems very cruel," Helen agreed. "He wasn't really fit to go back, but the Board passed him because they were so short of officers and he kept worrying them. He was so afraid he'd get moved to another battalion. Then he was taken prisoner in that horrible Pervais affair, and sent to the worst camp in Germany. Since then, of course, Philippa and I have had a wretched time, worrying."

"Major Felstead is Lady Cranston's only brother, is he not?" Griffiths enquired.

"And my only fiancé," she replied, with a little grimace. "However, don't let us talk about our troubles any more," she continued, with an effort at a lighter tone. "You'll find some cigarettes on that table, Mr. Harrison. I can't think where Nora is. I expect she has persuaded some one to take her out trophy-hunting to Dutchman's Common."

"The road all the way is like a circus," the young soldier observed, "and there isn't a thing to be seen when you get there. The naval airmen were all over the place at daybreak, and Captain Griffiths wasn't far behind them. You didn't leave much for the sightseers, sir," he concluded, turning to his neighbour.

"As Commandant of the place," Captain Griffiths replied, "I naturally had to have the Common searched. With the exception of the observation car, however, I think that I am betraying no confidences in telling you that we discovered nothing of interest."

"Do you suppose that the Zeppelin was in difficulties, as she was flying so low?" Helen enquired.

"It is a perfectly reasonable hypothesis," the Commandant assented. "Two patrol boats were sent out early this morning, in search of her. An old man whom I saw at Waburne declares that she passed like a long, black cloud, just over his head, and that he was almost deafened by the noise of the engines. Personally, I cannot believe that they would come down so low unless she was in some trouble."

The door of the comfortable library in which they were seated was suddenly thrown open. An exceedingly alert-looking young lady, very much befreckled, and as yet unemancipated from the long plaits of the schoolroom, came in like a whirlwind. In her hand she carried a man's Homburg hat, which she waved aloft in triumph.

"Come in, Arthur," she shouted to a young subaltern who was hovering in the background. "Look what I've got, Helen! A trophy! Just look, Mr. Harrison and Captain Griffiths! I found it in a bush, not twenty yards from where the observation car came down."

Helen turned the hat around in amused bewilderment.

"But, my dear child," she exclaimed, "this is nothing but an ordinary hat! People who travel in Zeppelins don't wear things like that. How do you do, Mr. Somerfield?" she added, smiling at the young man who had followed Nora into the room.

"Don't they!" the latter retorted, with an air of superior knowledge. "Just look here!"

She turned down the lining and showed it to them. "What do you make of that?" she asked triumphantly.

Helen gazed at the gold-printed letters a little incredulously.

"Read it out," Nora insisted.

Helen obeyed:

"Schmidt,
Berlin,
Unter den Linden, 127."

"That sounds German," she admitted.

"It's a trophy, all right," Nora declared. "One of the crew—probably the Commander—must have come on board in a hurry and changed into uniform after they had started."

"It is my painful duty, Miss Nora," Harrison announced solemnly, "to inform you, on behalf of Captain Griffiths, that all articles of whatsoever description, found in the vicinity of Dutchman's Common, which might possibly have belonged to any one in the Zeppelin, must be sent at once to the War Office."

"Rubbish!" Nora scoffed. "The War Office aren't going to have my hat."

"Duty," the young man began—

"You can go back to the Depot and do your duty, then, Mr. Harrison," Nora interrupted, "but you're not going to have my hat. I'd throw it into the fire sooner than give it up."

"Military regulations must be obeyed, Miss Nora," Captain Griffiths ventured thoughtfully.

"Nothing so important as hats," Harrison put in. "You see they fit—somebody."

The girl's gesture was irreverent but convincing. "I'd listen to anything Captain Griffiths had to say," she declared, "but you boys who are learning to be soldiers are simply eaten up with conceit. There's nothing in your textbook about hats. If you're going to make yourselves disagreeable about this, I shall simply ignore the regiment."

The two young men fell into attitudes of mock dismay. Nora took a chocolate from a box.

"Be merciful, Miss Nora!" Harrison pleaded tearfully.

"Don't break the regiment up altogether," Somerfield begged, with a little catch in his voice.

"All very well for you two to be funny," Nora went on, revisiting the chocolate box, "but you've heard about the Seaforths coming, haven't you? I adore kilts, and so does Helen; don't you, Helen?"

"Every woman does," Helen admitted, smiling. "I suppose the child really can keep the hat, can't she?" she added, turning to the Commandant.

"Officially the matter is outside my cognizance," he declared. "I shall have nothing to say."

The two young men exchanged glances.

"A hat," Somerfield ruminated, "especially a Homburg hat, is scarcely an appurtenance of warfare."

His brother officer stood for a moment looking gravely at the object in question. Then he winked at Somerfield and sighed.

"I shall take the whole responsibility," he decided magnanimously, "of saying nothing about the matter. We can't afford to quarrel with Miss Nora, can we, Somerfield?"

"Not on your life," that young man agreed.

"Sensible boys!" Nora pronounced graciously.

"Thank you very much, Captain Griffiths, for not encouraging them in their folly. You can take me as far as the post-office when you go, Arthur," she continued, turning to the fortunate possessor of the side-car, "and we'll have some golf to-morrow afternoon, if you like."

"Won't Mr. Somerfield have some tea?" Helen invited.

"Thank you very much, Miss Fairclough," the man replied; "we had tea some time ago at Watson's, where I found Miss Nora."

Nora suddenly held up her finger. "Isn't that the car?" she asked. "Why, it must be mummy, here already. Yes, I can hear her voice!"

Griffiths, who had moved eagerly towards the window, looked back.

"It is Lady Cranston," he announced solemnly.

CHAPTER II

The woman who paused for a moment upon the threshold of the library, looking in upon the little company, was undeniably beautiful. She had masses of red-gold hair, a little disordered by her long railway journey, deep-set hazel eyes, a delicate, almost porcelain-like complexion, and a sensitive, delightfully shaped mouth. Her figure was small and dainty, and just at that moment she had an appearance of helplessness which was almost childlike. Nora, after a vigorous embrace, led her stepmother towards a chair.

"Come and sit by the fire, Mummy," she begged. "You look tired and cold."

Philippa exchanged a general salutation with her guests. She was still wearing her travelling coat, and her air of fatigue was unmistakable. Griffiths, who had not taken his eyes off her since her entrance, wheeled an easy-chair towards the hearth-rug, into which she sank with a murmured word of thanks.

"You'll have some tea, won't you, dear?" Helen enquired.

Philippa shook her head. Her eyes met her friend's for a moment—it was only a very brief glance, but the tragedy of some mutual sorrow seemed curiously revealed in that unspoken question and answer. The two young subalterns prepared to take their leave. Nora, kneeling down, stroked her stepmother's hand.

"No news at all, then?" Helen faltered.

"None," was the weary reply.

"Any amount of news here, Mummy," Nora intervened cheerfully, "and heaps of excitement. We had a Zeppelin over Dutchman's Common last night, and she lost her observation car. Mr. Somerfield took me up there this afternoon, and I found a German hat. No one else got a thing, and, would you believe it, those children over there tried to take it away from me."

Her stepmother smiled faintly.

"I expect you are keeping the hat, dear," she observed.

"I should say so!" Nora assented.

Philippa held out her hand to the two young men who had been waiting to take their leave.

"You must come and dine one night this week, both of you," she said. "My husband will be home by the later train this evening, and I'm sure he will be glad to have you."

"Very kind of you, Lady Cranston, we shall be delighted," Harrison declared.

"Rather!" his companion echoed.

Nora led them away, and Helen, with a word of excuse, followed them. Griffiths, who had also risen to his feet, came a little nearer to Philippa's chair.

"And you, too, of course, Captain Griffiths," she said, smiling pleasantly up at him. "Must you hurry away?"

"I will stay, if I may, until Miss Fairclough returns," he answered, resuming his seat.

"Do!" Philippa begged him. "I have had such a miserable time in town. You can't think how restful it is to be back here."

"I am afraid," he observed, "that your journey has not been successful."

Philippa shook her head.

"It has been completely unsuccessful," she sighed. "I have not been able to hear a word about my brother. I am so sorry for poor Helen, too. They were only engaged, you know, a few days before he left for the front this last time."

Captain Griffiths nodded sympathetically.

"I never met Major Felstead," he remarked, "but every one who has seems to like him very much. He was doing so well, too, up to that last unfortunate affair, wasn't he?"

"Dick is a dear," Philippa declared. "I never knew any one with so many friends. He would have been commanding his battalion now, if only he were free. His colonel wrote and told me so himself."

"I wish there were something I could do," Griffiths murmured, a little awkwardly. "It hurts me, Lady Cranston, to see you so upset."

She looked at him for a moment in faint surprise.

"Nobody can do anything," she bemoaned. "That is the unfortunate part of it all."

He rose to his feet and was immediately conscious, as he always was when he stood up, that there was a foot or two of his figure which he had no idea what to do with.

"You wouldn't feel like a ride to-morrow morning, Lady Cranston?" he asked, with a wistfulness which seemed somehow stifled in his rather unpleasant voice. She shook her head.

"Perhaps one morning later," she replied, a little vaguely. "I haven't any heart for anything just now."

He took a sombre but agitated leave of his hostess, and went out into the twilight, cursing his lack of ease, remembering the things which he had meant to say, and hating himself for having forgotten them. Philippa, to whom his departure had been, as it always was, a relief, was already leaning forward in her chair with her arm around Helen's neck.

"I thought that extraordinary man would never go," she exclaimed, "and I was longing to send for you, Helen. London has been such a dreary chapter of disappointments."

"What a sickening time you must have had, dear!"

"It was horrid," Philippa assented sadly, "but you know Henry is no use at all, and I should have felt miserable unless I had gone. I have been to every friend at the War Office, and every friend who has friends there. I have made every sort of enquiry, and I know just as much now as I did when I left here—that Richard was a prisoner at Wittenberg the last time they heard, and that they have received no notification whatever concerning him for the last two months."

Helen glanced at the calendar.

"It is just two months to-day," she said mournfully, "since we heard."

"And then," Philippa sighed, "he hadn't received a single one of our parcels."

Helen rose suddenly to her feet. She was a tall, fair girl of the best Saxon type, slim but not in the least angular, with every promise, indeed, of a fuller and more gracious development in the years to come. She was barely twenty-two years old, and, as is common with girls of her complexion, seemed younger. Her bright, intelligent face was, above all, good-humoured. Just at that moment, however, there was a flush of passionate anger in her cheeks.

"It makes me feel almost beside myself," she exclaimed, "this hideous incapacity for doing anything! Here we are living in luxury, without a single privation, whilst Dick, the dearest thing on earth to both of us, is being starved and goaded to death in a foul German prison!"

"We mustn't believe that it's quite so bad as that, dear," Philippa remonstrated. "What is it, Mills?"

The elderly man-servant who had entered with a tray in his hand, bowed as he arranged it upon a side table.

"I have taken the liberty of bringing in a little fresh tea, your ladyship," he announced, "and some hot buttered toast. Cook has sent some of the sandwiches, too, which your ladyship generally fancies."

"It is very kind of you, Mills," Philippa said, with rather a wan little smile. "I had some tea at South Lynn, but it was very bad. You might take my coat, please."

She stood up, and the heavy fur coat slipped easily away from her slim, elegant little body.

"Shall I light up, your ladyship?" Mills enquired.

"You might light a lamp," Philippa directed, "but don't draw the blinds until lighting-up time. After the noise of London," she went on, turning to Helen, "I always think that the faint sound of the sea is so restful."

The man moved noiselessly about the room and returned once more to his mistress.

"We should be glad to hear, your ladyship," he said, "if there is any news of Major Felstead?" Philippa shook her head.

"None at all, I am sorry to say, Mills! Still, we must hope for the best. I dare say that some of these camps are not so bad as we imagine."

"We must hope not, your ladyship," was the somewhat dismal reply. "Shall I fasten the windows?"

"You can leave them until you draw the blinds, Mills," Philippa directed. "I am not at home, if any one should call. See that we are undisturbed for a little time."

"Very good, your ladyship."

The door was closed, and the two women were once more alone. Philippa held out her arms.

"Helen, darling, come and be nice to me," she begged. "Let us both pretend that no news is good news. Oh, I know what you are suffering, but remember that even if Dick is your lover, he is my dear, only brother—my twin brother, too. We have been so much to each other all our lives. He'll stick it out, dear, if any human being can. We shall have him back with us some day."

"But he is hungry," Helen sobbed. "I can't bear to think of his being hungry. Every time I sit down to eat, it almost chokes me."

"I suppose he has forgotten what a whisky and soda is like," Philippa murmured, with a little catch in her own throat.

"He always used to love one about this time," Helen faltered, glancing at the clock.

"And cigarettes!" Philippa exclaimed. "I wonder whether they give him anything to smoke."

"Nasty German tobacco, if they do," Helen rejoined indignantly. "And to think that I have sent him at least six hundred of his favourite Egyptians!"

She fell once more on her knees by her friend's side. Their arms were intertwined, their cheeks touching. One of those strange, feminine silences of acute sympathy seemed to hold them for a while under its thrall. Then, almost at the same moment, a queer awakening came for both of them. Helen's arm was stiffened. Philippa turned her head, but her eyes were filled with incredulous fear. A little current of cool air was blowing through the room. The French windows stood half open, and with his back to them, a man who had apparently entered the room from the gardens and passed noiselessly across the soft carpet, was standing by the door, listening. They heard him turn the key. Then, in a businesslike manner, he returned to the windows and closed them, the eyes of the two women following him all the time. Satisfied, apparently, with his precautions, he turned towards them just as an expression of indignant enquiry broke from Philippa's lips. Helen sprang to her feet, and Philippa gripped the sides of her chair. The newcomer advanced a few steps nearer to them

CHAPTER III

It seemed to the two women, brief though the period of actual silence was, that in those few seconds they jointly conceived definite and lasting impressions of the man who was to become, during the next few weeks, an object of the deepest concern to both of them. The intruder was slightly built, of little more than medium height, of dark complexion, with an almost imperceptible moustache of military pattern, black hair dishevelled with the wind, and eyes of almost peculiar brightness. He carried himself with an assurance which was somewhat remarkable considering the condition of his torn and mud stained clothes, the very quality of which was almost undistinguishable. They both, curiously enough, formed the same instinctive conviction that, notwithstanding his tramplike appearance and his burglarious entrance, this was not a person to be greatly feared.

The stranger brushed aside Philippa's incoherent exclamation and opened the conversation with some ceremony.

"Ladies," he began, with a low bow, "in the first place let me offer my most profound apologies for this unusual form of entrance to your house."

Philippa rose from her easy-chair and confronted him. The firelight played upon her red-gold hair, and surprise had driven the weariness from her face. Against the black oak of the chimneypiece she had almost the appearance of a framed cameo. Her voice was quite steady, although its inflection betrayed some indignation.

"Will you kindly explain who you are and what you mean by this extraordinary behaviour?" she demanded.

"It is my earnest intention to do so without delay," he assured her, his eyes apparently rivetted upon Philippa. "Kindly pardon me."

He held out his arm to stop Helen, who, with her eye upon the bell, had made a stealthy attempt to slip past him. Her eyes flashed as she felt his fingers upon her arm.

"How dare you attempt to stop me!" she exclaimed.

"My dear Miss Fairclough," he remonstrated, "in the interests of all of us, it is better that we should have a few moments of undisturbed conversation. I am taking it for granted that I have the pleasure of addressing Miss Fairclough?"

There was something about the man's easy confidence which was, in its way, impressive yet irritating. Helen appeared bereft of words and retreated to her place almost mildly. Philippa's very delicate eyebrows were drawn together in a slight frown.

"You are acquainted with our names, then?"

"Perfectly," was the suave reply. "You, I presume, are Lady Cranston? I may be permitted to add," he went on, looking at her steadfastly, "that the description from which I recognise you does you less than justice."

"I find that remark, under the circumstances, impertinent," Philippa told him coldly.

He shrugged his shoulders. There was a slight smile upon his lips and his eyes twinkled.

"Alas!" he murmured, "for the moment I forgot the somewhat unusual circumstances of our meeting. Permit me to offer you what I trust you will accept as the equivalent of a letter of introduction."

"A letter of introduction," Philippa repeated, glancing at his disordered clothes, "and you come in through the window!"

"Believe me," the intruder assured her, "it was the only way."

"Perhaps you will tell me, then," Philippa demanded, her anger gradually giving way to bewilderment, "what is wrong with my front door?"

"For all I know, dear lady," the newcomer confessed, "yours may be an excellent front door. I would ask you, however, to consider my appearance. I have been obliged to conclude the last few miles of my journey in somewhat ignominious fashion. My clothes—they were quite nice clothes, too, when I started," he added, looking down at himself ruefully—"have suffered. And, as you perceive, I have lost my hat."

"Your hat?" Helen exclaimed, with a sudden glance at Nora's trophy.

"Precisely! I might have posed before your butler, perhaps, as belonging to what you call the hatless brigade, but the mud upon my clothes, and these unfortunate rents in my garments, would have necessitated an explanation which I thought better avoided. I make myself quite clear, I trust?"

"Clear?" Philippa murmured helplessly.

"Clear?" Helen echoed, with a puzzled frown.

"I mean, of course," their visitor explained, "so far as regards my choosing this somewhat surreptitious form of entrance into your house."

Philippa shrugged her shoulders and made a determined move towards the bell. The intruder, however, barred her way. She looked up into his face and found it difficult to maintain her indignation. His expression, besides being distinctly pleasant, was full of a respectful admiration.

"Will you please let me pass?" she insisted.

"Madam," he replied, "I am afraid that it is your intention to ring the bell."

"Of course it is," she admitted. "Don't dare to prevent me."

"Madam, I do not wish to prevent you," he assured her. "A few moments' delay—that is all I plead for."

"Will you explain at once, sir," Philippa demanded, "what you mean by forcing your way into my house in this extraordinary fashion, and by locking that door?"

"I am most anxious to do so," was the prompt reply. "I am correct, of course, in my first surmise that you are Lady Cranston—and you Miss Fairclough?" he added, bowing ceremoniously to both of them. "A very great pleasure! I recognised you both quite easily, you see, from your descriptions."

"From our descriptions?" Philippa repeated.

The newcomer bowed.

"The descriptions, glowing, indeed, but by no means exaggerated, of your brother Richard, Lady Cranston, and your fiancé, Miss Fairclough."

"Richard?" Philippa almost shrieked.

"You have seen Dick?" Helen gasped.

The intruder dived in his pockets and produced two sealed envelopes. He handed one each simultaneously to Helen and to Philippa.

"My letters of introduction," he explained, with a little sigh of relief. "I trust that during their perusal you will invite me to have some tea. I am almost starving."

The two women hastened towards the lamp.

"One moment, I beg," their visitor interposed. "I have established, I trust, my credentials. May I remind you that I was compelled to ensure the safety of these few minutes' conversation with you, by locking that door. Are you likely to be disturbed?"

"No, no! No chance at all," Philippa assured him.

"If we are, we'll explain," Helen promised.

"In that case," the intruder begged, "perhaps you will excuse me."

He moved towards the door and softly turned the key, then he drew the curtains carefully across the French windows. Afterwards he made his way towards the tea-table. A little throbbing cry had broken from Helen's lips.

"Philippa," she exclaimed, "it's from Dick! It's Dick's handwriting!"

Philippa's reply was incoherent. She was tearing open her own envelope. With a well-satisfied smile, the bearer of these communications seized a sandwich in one hand and poured himself out some tea with the other. He ate and drank with the restraint of good-breeding, but with a voracity which gave point to his plea of starvation. A few yards away, the breathless silence between the two women had given place to an almost hysterical series of disjointed exclamations.

"It's from Dick!" Helen repeated. "It's his own dear handwriting. How shaky it is! He's alive and well, Philippa, and he's found a friend."

"I know—I know," Philippa murmured tremulously. "Our parcels have been discovered, and he got them all at once. Just fancy, Helen, he's really not so ill, after all!"

They drew a little closer together.

"You read yours out first," Helen proposed, "and then I'll read mine."

Philippa nodded. Her voice here and there was a little uncertain.

MY DEAREST SISTER,

I have heard nothing from you or Helen for so long that I was really getting desperate. I have had a very rough time here, but by the grace of Providence I stumbled up against an old friend the other day, Bertram Maderstrom, whom you must have

heard me speak of in my college days. It isn't too much to say that he has saved my life. He has unearthed your parcels, found me decent quarters, and I am getting double rations. He has promised, too, to get this letter through to you.

You needn't worry about me now, dear. I am feeling twice the man I was a month ago, and I shall stick it out now quite easily. Write me as often as ever you can. Your letters and Helen's make

all the difference.

My love to you and to Henry.

Your affectionate brother, RICHARD.

P.S. Is Henry an Admiral yet? I suppose he was in the Jutland scrap, which they all tell us here was a great German victory. I hope he came out all right.

Philippa read the postscript with a little shiver. Then she set her teeth as though determined to ignore it.

"Isn't it wonderful!" she exclaimed, turning towards Helen with glowing eyes. "Now yours, dear?"

Helen's voice trembled as she read. Her eyes, too, at times were misty:

DEAREST,

I am writing to you so differently because I feel that you will really get this letter. I have had an astonishing stroke of luck, as you will gather from Philippa's note. You can't imagine the difference. A month ago I really thought I should have to chuck

> it in. Now I am putting on flesh every day and beginning to feel myself again. I owe my life to a pal with whom I was at college, and whom you and I, dearest, will have to remember all our lives.
>
> I think of you always, and my thoughts are like the flowers of which we see nothing in these hideous huts. My greatest joy is in dreaming of the day when we shall meet again.
>
> Write to me often, sweetheart. Your letters and my thoughts of you are the one joy of my life.
>
> Always your lover,
DICK.

There were a few moments of significant silence. The girls were leaning together, their arms around one another's necks, their heads almost touching. Behind them, their visitor continued to eat and drink. He rose at last, however, reluctantly to his feet, and coughed. They started, suddenly remembering his presence. Philippa turned impulsively towards him with outstretched hands.

"I can't tell you how thankful we are to you," she declared.

"Both of us," Helen echoed.

He touched with his fingers a box of cigarettes which stood upon the tea-table.

"You permit?" he asked.

"Of course," Philippa assented eagerly. "You will find some matches on the tray there. Do please help yourself. I am afraid that I must have seemed very discourteous, but this has all been so amazing. Won't you have some fresh tea and some toast, or wouldn't you like some more sandwiches?"

"Nothing more at present, thank you," he replied. "If you do not mind, I would rather continue our conversation."

"These letters are wonderful," Philippa told him gratefully. "You know from whom they come, of course. Dick is my twin brother, and until the war we had scarcely ever been parted. Miss Fairclough here is engaged to be married to him. It is quite two months since we had a line, and I myself have been in London for the last three days, three very weary days, making enquiries everywhere."

"I am very happy," he said, "to have brought you such good news."

Once more the normal aspect of the situation began to reimpose itself upon the two women. They remembered the locked door, the secrecy of their visitor's entrance, and his disordered condition.

"May I ask to whom we are indebted for this great service?" Philippa enquired.

"My name for the present is Hamar Lessingham," was the suave reply.

"For the present?" Philippa repeated. "You have perhaps, some explanations to make," she went on, with some hesitation; "the condition of your clothes, your somewhat curious form of entrance?"

"With your permission."

"One moment," Helen intervened eagerly. "Is it possible, Mr. Lessingham, that you have seen Major Felstead lately?"

"A matter of fifty-six hours ago, Miss Fairclough. I am happy to tell you that he was looking, under the circumstances, quite reasonably well."

Helen caught up a photograph from the table by her side, and came over to their visitor's side.

"This was taken just before he went out the first time," she continued. "Is he anything like that now?"

Mr. Hamar Lessingham sighed and shook his head.

"You must expect," he warned her, "that prison and hospital have had their effect upon him. He was gaining strength every day, however, when I left."

Philippa held out her hand. She had been looking curiously at their visitor.

"Helen, dear, afterwards we will get Mr. Lessingham to talk to us about Dick," she insisted. "First there are some questions which I must ask."

He bowed slightly and drew himself up. For a moment it seemed as though they were entering upon a duel—the slight, beautiful woman and the man in rags.

"Just now," she began, "you told us that you saw Major Felstead, my brother, fifty-six hours ago."

"That is so," he assented.

"But it is impossible!" she pointed out. "My brother is a prisoner of war in Germany."

"Precisely," he replied, "and not, I am afraid, under the happiest conditions, he has been unfortunate in his camp. Let us talk about him, shall we?"

"Are you mad," Helen demanded, "or are you trying to confuse us?"

"My dear young lady!" he protested. "Why suppose such a thing? I was flattering myself that my conversation and deportment were, under the circumstances, perfectly rational."

"But you are talking nonsense," Philippa insisted. "You say that you saw Major Felstead fifty-six hours ago. You cannot mean us to believe that fifty-six hours ago you were at Wittenberg."

"That is precisely what I have been trying to tell you," he agreed.

"But it isn't possible!" Helen gasped.

"Quite, I assure you," he continued; "in fact, we should have been here before but for a little uncertainty as to your armaments along the coast. There was a gun, we were told, somewhere near here, which we were credibly informed had once been fired without the slightest accident."

Philippa's eyes seemed to grow larger and rounder.

"He's raving!" she decided.

"He isn't!" Helen cried, with sudden divination. "Is that your hat?" she asked, pointing to the table where Nora had left her trophy.

"It is," he admitted with a smile, "but I do not think that I will claim it."

"You were in the observation car of that Zeppelin!"

Lessingham extended his hand.

"Softly, please," he begged. "You have, I gather, arrived at the truth, but for the moment shall it be our secret? I made an exceedingly uncomfortable, not to say undignified descent from the Zeppelin which passed over Dutchman's Common last night."

"Then," Philippa cried, "you are a German!"

"My dear lady, I have escaped that misfortune," Lessingham confessed. "Do you think that none other than Germans ride in Zeppelins?"

CHAPTER IV

A new tenseness seemed to have crept into the situation. The conversation, never without its emotional tendencies, at once changed its character. Philippa, cold and reserved, with a threat lurking all the time in her tone and manner, became its guiding spirit.

"We may enquire your name?" she asked.

"I am the Baron Maderstrom," was the prompt reply. "For the purpose of my brief residence in this country, however, I fancy that the name of Mr. Hamar Lessingham might provoke less comment."

"Maderstrom," Philippa repeated. "You were at Magdalen with my brother."

"For three terms," he assented.

"You have visited at Wood Norton. It was only an accident, then, that I did not meet you."

"It is true," he answered, with a bow. "I received the most charming hospitality there from your father and mother."

"Why, you are the friend," Helen exclaimed, suddenly seizing his hands, "of whom Dick speaks in his letter!"

"It has been my great privilege to have been of service to Major Felstead," was the grave admission. "He and I, during our college days, were more than ordinarily intimate. I saw his name in one of the lists of prisoners, and I went at once to Wittenberg."

A fresh flood of questions was upon Helen's lips, but Philippa brushed her away.

"Please let me speak," she said. "You have brought us these letters from Richard, for which we offer you our heartfelt thanks, but you did not risk your liberty, perhaps your life, to come here simply as his ambassador. There is something beyond this in your visit to this country. You may be a Swede, but is it not true that at the present moment you are in the service of an enemy?"

Lessingham bowed acquiescence.

"You are entirely right," he murmured.

"Am I also right in concluding that you have some service to ask of us?"

"Your directness, dear lady, moves me to admiration," Lessingham assured her. "I am here to ask a trifling favour in return for those which I have rendered and those which I may yet render to your brother."

"And that favour?"

Their visitor looked down at his torn attire.

"A suit of your brother's clothes," he replied, "and a room in which to change. The disposal of these rags I may leave, I presume, to your ingenuity."

"Anything else?"

"It is my wish," he continued, "to remain in this neighbourhood for a short time—perhaps a fortnight and perhaps a month. I should value your introduction to the hotel here, and the extension of such hospitality as may seem fitting to you, under the circumstances."

"As Mr. Hamar Lessingham?"

"Beyond a doubt."

There was a moment's silence. Philippa's face had become almost stony. She took a step towards the telephone. Lessingham, however, held out his hand.

"Your purpose?" he enquired.

"I am going to ring up the Commandant here," she told him, "and explain your presence in this house."

"An heroic impulse," he observed, "but too impulsive."

"We shall see," she retorted. "Will you let me pass?"

His fingers restrained her as gently as possible.

"Let me make a reasonable appeal to both of you," he suggested. "I am here at your mercy. I promise you that under no circumstances will I attempt any measure of violence. From any fear of that, I trust my name and my friendship with your brother will be sufficient guarantee."

"Continue, then," Philippa assented.

"You will give me ten minutes in which to state my case," he begged.

"We must!" Helen exclaimed. "We must, Philippa! Please!"

"You shall have your ten minutes," Philippa conceded.

He abandoned his attitude of watchfulness and moved back on to the hearth-rug, his hands behind him. He addressed himself to Philippa. It was Philippa who had become his judge.

"I will claim nothing from you," he began, "for the services which I have rendered to Richard. Our friendship was a real thing, and, finding him in such straits, I would gladly, under any circumstances, have done all that I have done. I am well paid for this by the thanks which you have already proffered me."

"No thanks—nothing that we could do for you would be sufficient recompense," Helen declared energetically.

"Let me speak for a moment of the future," he continued. "Supposing you ring that telephone and hand me over to the authorities here? Well, that will be the end of me, without a doubt. You will have done what seemed to you to be the right thing, and I hope that that consciousness will sustain you, for, believe me, though it may not be at my will, your brother's life will most certainly answer for mine."

There was a slight pause. A sob broke from Helen's throat. Even Philippa's lip quivered.

"Forgive me," he went on, "if that sounds like a threat. It was not so meant. It is the simple truth. Let me hurry on to the future. I ask so little of you. It is my duty to live in this spot for one month. What harm can I do? You have no great concentration of soldiers here, no docks, no fortifications, no industry. And in return for the slight service of allowing me to remain here unmolested, I pledge my word that Richard shall be set at liberty and shall be here with you within two months."

Helen's face was transformed, her eyes glowed, her lips were parted with eagerness. She turned towards Philippa, her expression, her whole attitude an epitome of eloquent pleading.

"Philippa, you will not hesitate? You cannot?"

"I must," Philippa answered, struggling with her agitation. "I love Dick more dearly than anything else on earth, but just now, Helen, we have to remember, before everything, that we are English women. We have to put our human feelings behind us. We are learning every day to make sacrifices. You, too, must learn, dear. My answer to you, Baron Maderstrom—or Mr. Lessingham, as you choose to call yourself—is no."

"Philippa, you are mad!" Helen exclaimed passionately. "Didn't I have to realise all that you say when I let Dick go, cheerfully, the day after we were engaged? Haven't I realised the duty of cheerfulness and sacrifice through all these weary months? But there is a limit to these things, Philippa, a sense of proportion which must be taken into account. It's Dick's life which is in the balance against some intangible thing, nothing that we could ever reproach ourselves with, nothing that could bring real harm upon any one. Oh, I love my country, too, but I want Dick! I should feel like his murderess all my life, if I didn't consent!"

"It occurs to me," Lessingham remarked, turning towards Philippa, "that Miss Fairclough's point of view is one to be considered."

"Doesn't all that Miss Fairclough has said apply to me?" Philippa demanded, with a little break in her voice. "Richard is my twin brother, he is the dearest thing in life to me. Can't you realise, though, that what you ask of us is treason?"

"It really doesn't amount to that," Lessingham assured her. "In my own heart I feel convinced that I have come here on a fool's errand. No object that I could possibly attain in this neighbourhood is worth the life of a man like Richard Felstead."

"Oh, he's right!" Helen exclaimed. "Think, Philippa! What is there here which the whole world might not know? There are no secrets in Dreymarsh. We are miles away from everywhere. For my sake, Philippa, I implore you not to be unreasonable."

"In plain words," Lessingham intervened, "do not be quixotic, Lady Cranston. There is just an idea on one side, your brother's life on the other. You see, the scales do not balance."

"Can't you realise, though," Philippa answered, "what that idea means? It is part of one's soul that one gives when one departs from a principle."

"What are principles against love?" Helen demanded, almost fiercely. "A sister may prate about them, Philippa. A wife couldn't. I'd sacrifice every principle I ever had, every scrap of self-respect, myself and all that belongs to me, to save Dick's life!"

There was a brief, throbbing silence. Helen was feverishly clutching Philippa's hand. Lessingham's eyes were fixed upon the tortured face into which he gazed. There were no women like this in his own country.

"Dear lady," he said, and for the first time his own voice shook, "I abandon my arguments. I beg you to act as you think best for your own future happiness. The chances of life or death are not great things for either men like your brother or for me. I would not purchase my end, nor he his life, at the expense of your suffering. You see, I stand on one side. The telephone is there for your use."

"You shan't use it!" Helen cried passionately. "Phillipa, you shan't!"

Philippa turned towards her, and all the stubborn pride had gone out of her face. Her great eyes were misty with tears, her mouth was twitching with emotion. She threw her arms around Helen's neck.

"My dear, I can't! I can't!" she sobbed.

CHAPTER V

Philippa's breakdown was only momentary. With a few brusque words she brought the other two down to the level of her newly recovered equanimity.

"To be practical," she began, "we have no time to lose. I will go and get a suit of Dick's clothes, and, Helen, you had better take Mr. Lessingham into the gun room. Afterwards, perhaps you will have time to ring up the hotel."

Lessingham took a quick step towards her,—almost as though he were about to make some impetuous withdrawal. Philippa turned and met his almost pleading gaze. Perhaps she read there his instinct of self-abnegation.

"I am in command of the situation," she continued, a little more lightly. "Every one must please obey me. I shan't be more than five minutes."

She left the room, waving back Lessingham's attempt to open the door for her. He stood for a moment looking at the place where she had vanished. Then he turned round.

"Major Felstead's description," he said quietly, "did not do his sister justice."

"Philippa is a dear," Helen declared enthusiastically. "Just for a moment, though, I was terrified. She has a wonderful will."

"How long has she been married?"

"About six years."

"Are there—any children?"

Helen shook her head.

"Sir Henry had a daughter by his first wife, who lives with us."

"Six years!" Lessingham repeated. "Why, she seems no more than a child. Sir Henry must be a great deal her senior."

"Sixteen years," Helen told him. "Philippa is twenty-nine. And now, don't be inquisitive any more, please, and come with me. I want to show you where to change your clothes."

She opened a door on the other side of the room, and pointed to a small apartment across the passage.

"If you'll wait in there," she begged, "I'll bring the clothes to you directly they come. I am going to telephone now."

"So many thanks," he answered. "I should like a pleasant bedroom and sitting room, and a bathroom if possible. My luggage you will find already there. A friend in London has seen to that."

She looked at him curiously.

"You are very thorough, aren't you?" she remarked.

"The people of the country whom it is my destiny to serve all are," he replied. "One weak link, you know, may sometimes spoil the mightiest chain."

She closed the door and took up the telephone.

"Number three, please," she began. "Are you the hotel? The manager? Good! I am speaking for Lady Cranston. She wishes a sitting-room, bedroom and bath-room reserved for a friend of ours who is arriving to-day—a Mr. Hamar Lessingham. You have his luggage already, I believe. Please do the best you can for him.—Certainly.—Thank you very much."

She set down the receiver. The door was quickly opened and shut. Philippa reappeared, carrying an armful of clothes.

"Why, you've brought his grey suit," Helen cried in dismay, "the one he looks so well in!"

"Don't be an idiot," Philippa scoffed. "I had to bring the first I could find. Take them in to Mr. Lessingham, and for heaven's sake see that he hurries! Henry's train is due, and he may be here at any moment."

"I'll tell him," Helen promised. "I'll smuggle him out of the back way, if you like."

Philippa laughed a little drearily.

"A nice start that would be, if any one ever traced his arrival!" she observed. "No, we must try and get him away before Henry comes, but, if the worst comes to the worst, we'll have him in and introduce him. Henry isn't likely to notice anything," she added, a little bitterly.

Helen disappeared with the clothes and returned almost immediately, Philippa was sitting in her old position by the fire.

"You're not worrying about this, dear, are you?" the former asked anxiously.

"I don't know," Philippa replied, without turning her head. "I don't know what may come of it, Helen. I have a queer sort of feeling about that man."

Helen sighed. "I suppose," she confessed, "I am the narrowest person on earth. I can think of one thing, and one thing only. If Mr. Lessingham keeps his word, Dick will be here perhaps in a month, perhaps six weeks—certainly soon!"

"He will keep his word," Philippa said quietly. "He is that sort of man."

The door on the other side of the room was softly opened. Lessingham's head appeared.

"Could I have a necktie?" he asked diffidently. Philippa stretched out her hand and took one from the basket by her side.

"Better give him this," she said, handing it over to Helen. "It is one of Henry's which I was mending.—Stop!"

She put up her finger. They all listened.

"The car!" Philippa exclaimed, rising hastily to her feet. "That is Henry! Go out with Mr. Lessingham, Helen," she continued, "and wait until he is ready. Don't forget that he is an ordinary caller, and bring him in presently."

Helen nodded understandingly and hurried out.

Philippa moved a few steps towards the other door. In a moment it was thrown open. Nora appeared, with her arm through her father's.

"I went to meet him, Mummy," she explained. "No uniform—isn't it a shame!"

Sir Henry patted her cheek and turned to greet his wife. There was a shadow upon his bronzed, handsome face as he watched her rather hesitating approach.

"Sorry I couldn't catch your train, Phil," he told her. "I had to make a call in the city so I came down from Liverpool Street. Any luck?"

She held his hands, resisting for the moment his proffered embrace.

"Henry," she said earnestly, "do you know I am so much more anxious to hear your news."

"Mine will keep," he replied. "What about Richard?"

She shook her head.

"I spent the whole of my time making enquiries," she sighed, "and every one was fruitless. I failed to get the least satisfaction from any one at the War Office. They know nothing, have heard nothing."

"I'm ever so sorry to hear it," Sir Henry declared sympathetically. "You mustn't worry too much, though, dear. Where's Helen?"

"She is in the gun room with a caller."

"With a caller?" Nora exclaimed. "Is it any one from the Depot? I must go and see."

"You needn't trouble," her stepmother replied. "Here they are, coming in."

The door on the opposite side of the room was suddenly opened, and Hamar Lessingham and Helen entered together. Lessingham was entirely at his ease,—their conversation, indeed, seemed almost engrossing. He came at once across the room on realising Sir Henry's presence.

"This is Mr. Hamar Lessingham—my husband," Philippa said. "Mr. Lessingham was at college with Dick, Henry, so of course Helen and he have been indulging in all sorts of reminiscences."

The two men shook hands.

"I found time also to examine your Leech prints," Lessingham remarked. "You have some very admirable examples."

"Quite a hobby of mine in my younger days," Sir Henry admitted. "One or two of them are very good, I believe. Are you staying in these parts long, Mr. Lessingham?"

"Perhaps for a week or two," was the somewhat indifferent reply. "I am told that this is the most wonderful air in the world, so I have come down here to pull up again after a slight illness."

"A dreary spot just now," Sir Henry observed, "but the air's all right. Are you a sea-fisherman, by any chance, Mr. Lessingham?"

"I have done a little of it," the visitor confessed. Sir Henry's face lit up. He drew from his pocket a small, brown paper parcel.

"I don't mind telling you," he confided as he cut the string, "that I don't think there's another sport like it in the world. I have tried most of them, too. When I was a boy I was all for shooting, perhaps because I could never get enough. Then I had a season or two at Melton, though I was never much of a horseman. But for real, unadulterated excitement, for sport that licks everything else into a cocked hat, give me a strong sea rod, a couple of traces, just enough sea to keep on the bottom all the time, and the codling biting. Look here, did you ever see a mackerel spinner like that?" he added, drawing one out of the parcel which he had untied. "Look at it, all of you."

Lessingham took it gingerly in his fingers. Philippa, a little ostentatiously, turned her back upon the two men and took up a newspaper.

"Lady Cranston does not sympathize with my interest in any sort of sport just now," Sir Henry explained good-humouredly. "All the same I argue that one must keep one's mind occupied somehow or other."

"Quite right, Dad!" Nora agreed. "We must carry on, as the Colonel says. All the same, I did hope you'd come down in a new naval uniform, with lots of gold braid on your sleeve. I think they might have made you an admiral, Daddy, you'd look so nice on the bridge."

"I am afraid," her father replied, with his eyes glued upon the spinner which Lessingham was holding, "that that is a consideration which didn't seem to weigh with them much. Look at the glitter of it," he went on, taking up another of the spinners. "You see, it's got a double swivel, and they guarantee six hundred revolutions a minute."

"I must plead ignorance," Lessingham regretted, "of everything connected with mackerel spinning."

"It's fine sport for a change," Sir Henry declared. "The only thing is that if you strike a shoal one gets tired of hauling the beggars in. By-the-by, has Jimmy been up for me, Philippa? Have you heard whether there are any mackerel in?"

Philippa raised her eyebrows.

"Mackerel!" she repeated sarcastically.

"Have you any objection to the fish, dear?" Sir Henry enquired blandly.

Philippa made no reply. Her husband frowned and turned towards Lessingham.

"You see," he complained a little irritably, "my wife doesn't approve of my taking an interest even in fishing while the war's on, but, hang it all, what are you to do when you reach my age? Thinks I ought to be a special constable, don't you, Philippa?"

"Need we discuss this before Mr. Lessingham?" she asked, without looking up from her paper.

Lessingham promptly prepared to take his departure.

"See something more of you, I hope," Sir Henry remarked hospitably, as he conducted his guest to the door. "Where are you staying here?"

"At the hotel."

"Which?"

"I did not understand that there was more than one," Lessingham replied. "I simply wrote to The Hotel, Dreymarsh."

"There is only one hotel open, of course, Mr. Lessingham," Philippa observed, turning towards him. "Why do you ask such an absurd question, Henry? The 'Grand' is full of soldiers. Come and see us whenever you feel inclined, Mr. Lessingham."

"I shall certainly take advantage of your permission, Lady Cranston," were the farewell words of this unusual visitor as he bowed himself out.

Sir Henry moved to the sideboard and helped himself to a whisky and soda. Philippa laid down her newspaper and watched him as though waiting patiently for his return. Helen and Nora had already obeyed the summons of the dressing bell.

"Henry, I want to hear your news," she insisted. He threw himself into an easy-chair and turned over the contents of Philippa's workbasket.

"Where's that tie of mine you were mending?" he asked. "Is it finished yet?"

"It is upstairs somewhere," she replied. "No, I have not finished it. Why do you ask? You have plenty, haven't you?"

"Drawers full," he admitted cheerfully. "Half of them I can never wear, though. I like that black and white fellow. Your friend Lessingham was wearing one exactly like it."

"It isn't exactly an uncommon pattern," Philippa reminded him.

"Seems to have the family taste in clothes," Sir Henry continued, stroking his chin. "That grey tweed suit of his was exactly the same pattern as the suit Richard was wearing, the last time I saw him in mufti."

"They probably go to the same tailor," Philippa remarked equably.

Sir Henry abandoned the subject. He was once more engrossed in an examination of the mackerel spinners.

"You didn't answer my question about Jimmy Dumble," he ventured presently.

Philippa turned and looked at him. Her eyes were usually very sweet and soft and her mouth delightful. Just at that moment, however, there were new and very firm lines in her face.

"Henry," she said sternly, "you are purposely fencing with me. Mr. Lessingham's taste in clothes, or Jimmy Dumble's comings and goings, are not what I want to hear or talk about. You went to London, unwillingly enough, to keep your promise to me. I want to know whether you have succeeded in getting anything from the Admiralty?"

"Nothing but the cold shoulder, my dear," he answered with a little chuckle.

"Do you mean to say that they offered you nothing at all?" she persisted. "You may have been out of the service too long for them to start you with a modern ship, but surely they could have given you an auxiliary cruiser, or a secondary command of some sort?"

"They didn't even offer me a washtub, dear," he confessed. "My name's on a list, they said—"

"Oh, that list!" Philippa interrupted angrily. "Henry, I really can't bear it. Couldn't they find you anything on land?"

"My dear girl," he replied a little testily, "what sort of a figure should I cut in an office! No one can read my writing, and I couldn't add up a column of figures to save my life. What is it?" he added, as the door opened, and Mills made his appearance.

"Dumble is here to see you, sir."

"Show him in at once," his master directed with alacrity. "Come in, Jimmy," he went on, raising his voice. "I've got something to show you here."

Philippa's lips were drawn a little closer together. She swept past her husband on her way to the door.

"I hope you will be so good," she said, looking back, "as to spare me half an hour of your valuable time this evening. This is a subject which I must discuss with you further at once."

"As urgent as all that, eh?" Sir Henry replied, stopping to light a cigarette. "Righto! You can have the whole of my evening, dear, with the greatest of pleasure.—Now then, Jimmy!"

CHAPTER VI

Jimmy Dumble possessed a very red face and an extraordinary capacity for silence. He stood a yard or two inside the room, twirling his hat in his hand. Sir Henry, after the closing of the door, did not for a moment address his visitor. There was a subtle but unmistakable change in his appearance as he stood with his hands in his pockets, and a frown on his forehead, whistling softly to himself, his eyes fixed upon the door through which his wife had vanished. He swung round at last towards the telephone.

"Stand by for a moment, Jimmy, will you?" he directed.

"Aye, aye, sir!"

Sir Henry took up the receiver. He dropped his voice a little, although it was none the less distinct.

"Number one—police-station, please.—Hullo there! The inspector about?—That you, Inspector?—Sir Henry Cranston speaking. Could you just step round?—Good! Tell them to show you straight into the library. You might just drop a hint to Mills about the lights, eh? Thank you."

He laid down the receiver and turned towards the fisherman.

"Well, Jimmy," he enquired, "all serene down in the village, eh?"

"So far as I've seen or heard, sir, there ain't been a word spoke as shouldn't be."

"A lazy lot they are," Sir Henry observed.

"They don't look far beyond the end of their noses."

"Maybe it's as well for us, sir, as they don't," was the cautious reply.

Sir Henry strolled to the further end of the room.

"Perhaps you are right, Jimmy," he admitted.

"That fellow Ben Oates seems to be the only one with ideas."

"He don't keep sober long enough to give us any trouble," Dumble declared. "He began asking me questions a few days ago, and I know he put Grice's lad on to find out which way we went last Saturday week, but that don't amount to anything. He was dead drunk for three days afterwards."

Sir Henry nodded.

"I'm not very frightened of Ben Oates, Jimmy," he confided, as he threw open the door of a large cabinet which stood against the further wall. "No strangers about, eh?"

"Not a sign of one, sir."

Sir Henry glanced towards the door and listened.

"Shall I just give the key a turn, sir?" his visitor asked.

"I don't think it is necessary," Sir Henry replied. "They've all gone up to change. Now listen to me, Jimmy."

He leaned forward and touched a spring. The false back of the cabinet, with its little array of flies, spinners, fishing hooks and tackle, slowly rolled back. Before them stood a huge chart, wonderfully executed in red, white and yellow.

"That's a marvellous piece of work, sir," the fisherman observed admiringly.

"Best thing I ever did in my life," Sir Henry agreed. "Now see here, Jimmy. We'll sail out tomorrow, or take the motor boat, according to the wind. We'll enter Langley Shallows there and pass Dead Man's Rock on the left side of the waterway, and keep straight on until we get Budden Wood on the church tower. You follow me?"

"Aye, aye, sir!"

"We make for the headland from there. You see, we shall be outside the Gidney Shallows, and number twelve will pick us up. Put all the fishing tackle in the boat, and don't forget the bait. We must never lose sight of the fact, Jimmy, that the main object of our lives is to catch fish."

"That's right, sir," was the hearty assent.

"We'll be off at seven o'clock sharp, then," Sir Henry decided.

"The tide'll be on the flow by that time," Jimmy observed, "and we'll get off from the staith breakwater. That do be a fine piece of work and no mistake," he added, as the false back of the cabinet glided slowly to its place.

Sir Henry chuckled.

"It's nothing to the one I've got on number twelve, Jimmy," he said. "I've got the seaweed on that, pretty well. You'll take a drop of whisky on your way out?" he added. "Mills will look after you."

"I thank you kindly, sir."

Mills answered the bell with some concern in his face.

"The inspector is here to see you, sir," he announced. "He did mention something about the lights. I'm sure we've all been most careful. Even her ladyship has only used a candle in her bedroom."

"Show the inspector in," Sir Henry directed, "and I'll hear what he has to say. And give Dumble some whisky as he goes out, and a cigar."

"Wishing you good night, sir," the latter said, as he followed Mills. "I'll be punctual in the morning. Looks to me as though we might have good sport."

"We'll hope for it, anyway, Jimmy," his employer replied cheerfully. "Come in, Inspector."

The inspector, a tall, broad-shouldered man, saluted and stood at attention. Sir Henry nodded affably and glanced towards the door. He remained silent until Mills and Dumble had disappeared.

"Glad I happened to catch you, Inspector," he observed, sitting on the edge of the table and helping himself to another cigarette. "Any fresh arrivals?"

"None, sir," the man reported, "of any consequence that I can see. There are two more young officers for the Depot, and the young lady for the Grange, and Mr. and Mrs. Silvester returned home last night. There was a commercial traveller came in the first train this morning, but he went on during the afternoon."

"Hm! What about a Mr. Lessingham—a Mr. Hamar Lessingham?"

"I haven't heard of him, sir."

"Have you had the registration papers down from the hotel yet?"

"Not this evening, sir. I met the Midland and Great Northern train in myself. Her ladyship was the only passenger to alight here."

"And I came the other way myself," Sir Henry reflected.

"Now you come to mention the matter, sir," the inspector continued, "I was up at the hotel this afternoon, and I saw some luggage about addressed to a name somewhat similar to that."

"Probably sent on in advance, eh?"

"There could be no other way, sir," the inspector replied, "unless the registration paper has been mislaid. I'll step up to the hotel this evening and make sure."

"You'll oblige me very much, if you will. By Jove," Sir Henry added, looking towards the door, "I'd no idea it was so late!"

Philippa, who had changed her travelling dress for a plain black net gown, was standing in the doorway. She looked at the inspector, and for a moment the little colour which she had seemed to disappear.

"Is anything the matter?" she asked breathlessly.

"Nothing in the world, my dear," her husband assured her. "I am frightfully sorry I'm so late. Jimmy stayed some time, and then the inspector here looked in about our lights. Just a little more care in this room at night, he thinks. We'll see to it, Inspector."

"I am very much obliged, sir," the man replied. "Sorry to be under the necessity of mentioning it."

Sir Henry opened the door.

"You'll find your own way out, won't you?" he begged. "I'm a little late."

The inspector saluted and withdrew. Sir Henry glanced round.

"I won't be ten minutes, Philippa," he promised. "I had no idea it was so late."

"Come here one moment, please," she insisted.

He came back into the room and stood on the other side of the small table near which she had paused.

"What is it, dear?" he enquired. "We are going to leave our talk till after dinner, aren't we?"

She looked him in the face. There was an anxious light in her eyes, and she was certainly not herself. "Of course! I only wanted to know—it seemed to me that you broke off in what you were saying to the inspector, as I came into the room. Are you sure that it was the lights he came around about? There isn't anything else wrong, is there?"

"What else could there be?" he asked wonderingly.

"I have no idea," she replied, with well-simulated indifference. "I was only asking you whether there was anything else?"

He shook his head.

"Nothing!"

She threw herself into an easy-chair and picked up a magazine. "Thank you," she said. "Do hurry, please. I have a new cook and she asked particularly whether we were punctual people."

"Six minutes will see me through it," Sir Henry promised, making for the door. "Come to think of it, I missed my lunch. I think I'll manage it in five."

CHAPTER VII

Sir Henry was in a pleasant and expansive humour that evening. The new cook was an unqualified success, and he was conscious of having dined exceedingly well. He sat in a comfortable easy-chair before a blazing wood fire, he had just lit one of his favourite brand of cigarettes, and his wife, whom he adored, was seated only a few feet away.

"Quite a remarkable change in Helen," he observed. "She was in the depths of depression when I went away, and to-night she seems positively cheerful."

"Helen varies a great deal," Philippa reminded him.

"Still, to-night, I must say, I should have expected to have found her more depressed than ever," Sir Henry went on. "She hoped so much from your trip to London, and you apparently accomplished nothing."

"Nothing at all."

"And you have had no letters?"

"None."

"Then Helen's high spirits, I suppose, are only part of woman's natural inconsistency.—Philippa, dear!"

"Yes?"

"I am glad to be at home. I am glad to see you sitting there. I know you are nursing up something, some little thunderbolt to launch at me. Won't you launch it and let's get it over?"

Philippa laid down the book which she had been reading, and turned to face her husband. He made a little grimace.

"Don't look so severe," he begged. "You frighten me before you begin."

"I'm sorry," she said, "but my face probably reflects my feelings. I am hurt and grieved and disappointed in you, Henry."

"That's a good start, anyway," he groaned.

"We have been married six years," Philippa went on, "and I admit at once that I have been very happy. Then the war came. You know quite well, Henry, that especially at that time I was very, very fond of you, yet it never occurred to me for a moment but that, like every other woman, I should have to lose my husband for a time.—Stop, please," she insisted, as he showed signs of interrupting. "I know quite well that it was through my persuasions you retired so early, but in those days there was no thought of war, and I always had it in my mind that if trouble came you would find your way back to where you belonged."

"But, my dear child, that is all very well," Sir Henry protested, "but it's not so easy to get back again. You know very well that I went up to the Admiralty and offered my services, directly the war started."

"Yes, and what happened?" Philippa demanded. "You were, in a measure, shelved. You were put on a list and told that you would hear from them—a sort of Micawber-like situation with which you were perfectly satisfied. Then you took that moor up in Scotland and disappeared for nearly six months."

"I was supplying the starving population with food," he reminded her genially. "We sent about four hundred brace of grouse to market, not to speak of the salmon. We had some very fair golf, too, some of the time."

"Oh, I have not troubled to keep any exact account of your diversions!" Philippa said scornfully. "Sometimes," she continued, "I wonder whether you are quite responsible, Henry. How you can even talk of these things when every man of your age and strength is fighting one way or another for his country, seems marvellous to me. Do you realise that we are fighting for our very existence? Do you realise that my own father, who is fifteen years older than you, is in the firing line? This is a small place, of course, but there isn't a man left in it of your age, with your physique, who has had the slightest experience in either service, who isn't doing something."

"I can't do more than send in applications," he grumbled. "Be reasonable, my dear Philippa. It isn't the easiest thing in the world to find a job for a sailor who has been out of it as long as I have."

"So you say, but when they ask me what you are doing, as they all did in London this time, and I reply that you can't get a job, there is generally a polite little silence. No one believes it. I don't believe it."

"Philippa!"

Sir Henry turned in his chair. His cigar was burning now idly between his fingers. His heavy eyebrows were drawn together.

"Well, I don't," she reiterated. "You can be angry, if you will—in fact I think I should prefer you to be angry. You take no pains at the Admiralty. You just go there and come away again, once a year or something like that. Why, if I were you, I wouldn't leave the place until they'd found me something—indoors or outdoors, what does it matter so long as your hand is on the wheel and you are doing your little for your country? But you—what do you care? You went to town to get a job—and you come back with new mackerel spinners! You are off fishing to-morrow morning with Jimmy Dumble. Somewhere up in the North Sea, to-day and to-morrow and the next day, men are giving their lives for their country. What do you care? You will sit there smoking your pipe and catching dabs!"

"Do you know you are almost offensive, Philippa?" her husband said quietly.

"I want to be," she retorted. "I should like you to feel that I am. In any case, this will probably be the last conversation I shall hold with you on the subject."

"Well, thank God for that, anyway!" he observed, strolling to the chimneypiece and selecting a pipe from a rack. "I think you've said about enough."

"I haven't finished," she told him ominously.

"Then for heaven's sake get on with it and let's have it over," he begged.

"Oh, you're impossible!" Philippa exclaimed bitterly. "Listen. I give you one chance more. Tell me the truth? Is there anything in your health of which I do not know? Is there any possible explanation of your extraordinary behaviour which, for some reason or other, you have kept to yourself? Give me your whole confidence."

Sir Henry, for a moment, was serious enough. He stood looking down at her a little wistfully.

"My dear," he told her, "I have nothing to say except this. You are my very precious wife. I have loved you and trusted you since the day of our marriage. I am content to go on loving and trusting you, even though things should come under my notice which I do not understand. Can't you accept me the same way?"

Philippa, momentarily uneasy, was nevertheless rebellious.

"Accept you the same way? How can I! There is nothing in my life to compare in any way with the tragedy of your—"

She paused, as though unwilling to finish the sentence. He waited patiently, however, for her to proceed.

"Of my what?"

Philippa compromised.

"Lethargy," she pronounced triumphantly.

"An excellent word," he murmured.

"It is too mild a one, but you are my husband," she remarked.

"That reminds me," he said quietly. "You are my wife."

"I know it," she admitted, "but I am also a woman, and there are limits to my endurance. If you can give me no explanation of your behaviour, Henry, if you really have no intention of changing it, then there is only one course left open for me."

"That sounds rather alarming—what is it?" he demanded.

Philippa lifted her head a little. This was the pronouncement towards which she had been leading.

"From to-day," she declared, "I cease to be your wife."

His fingers paused in the manipulation of the tobacco with which he was filling his pipe. He turned and looked at her.

"You what?"

"I cease to be your wife."

"How do you manage that?" he asked.

"Don't jest," she begged. "It hurts me so. What I mean is surely plain enough. I will continue to live under your roof if you wish it, or I am perfectly willing to go back to Wood Norton. I will continue to bear your name because I must, but the other ties between us are finished."

"You don't mean this, Philippa," he said gravely.

"But I do mean it," she insisted. "I mean every word I have spoken. So far as I am concerned, Henry, this is your last chance."

There was a knock at the door. Mills entered with a note upon a salver. Sir Henry took it up, glanced questioningly at his wife, and tore open the envelope.

"There will be no answer, Mills," he said.

The man withdrew. Sir Henry read the few lines thoughtfully:—

Police-station, Dreymarsh

SIR,

According to enquiries made I find that Mr. Hamar Lessingham arrived at the Hotel this evening in time for dinner. His luggage arrived by rail yesterday. It is presumed that he came by motor-car, but there is no car in the garage, nor any mention of one. His room was taken for him by Miss Fairclough, ringing up for Lady Cranston about seven o'clock.

Respectfully yours,
JOHN HAYLOCK.

"Is your note of interest?" Philippa enquired.

"In a sense, yes," he replied, thrusting it into his waistcoat pocket. "I presume we can consider our late subject of conversation finished with?"

"I have nothing more to say," she pronounced.

"Very well, then," her husband agreed, "let us select another topic. This time, supposing I choose?"

"You are welcome."

"Let us converse, then, about Mr. Hamar Lessingham."

Philippa had taken up her work. Her fingers ceased their labours, but she did not look up.

"About Mr. Hamar Lessingham," she repeated. "Rather a limited subject, I am afraid."

"I am not so sure," he said thoughtfully. "For instance, who is he?"

"I have no idea," she replied. "Does it matter? He was at college with Richard, and he has been a visitor at Wood Norton. That is all that we know. Surely it is sufficient for us to offer him any reasonable hospitality?"

"I am not disputing it," Sir Henry assured her. "On the face of it, it seems perfectly reasonable that you should be civil to him. On the other hand, there are one or two rather curious points about his coming here just now."

"Really?" Philippa murmured indifferently, bending a little lower over her work.

"In the first place," her husband continued, "how did he arrive here?"

"For all I know," she replied, "he may have walked."

"A little unlikely. Still, he didn't come from London by either of the evening trains, and it seems that you didn't take his rooms for him until about seven o'clock, before which time he hadn't been to the hotel. So, you see, one is driven to wonder how the mischief he did get here."

"I took his rooms?" Philippa repeated, with a sudden little catch at her heart.

"Some one from here rang up, didn't they?" Sir Henry went on carelessly. "I gathered that we were introducing him at the hotel."

"Where did you hear that?" she demanded.

He shrugged his shoulders, but avoided answering the question.

"I have no doubt," he continued, "that the whole subject of Mr. Hamar Lessingham is scarcely worth discussing. Yet he does seem to have arrived here under a little halo of coincidence."

"I am afraid I have scarcely appreciated that," Philippa remarked; "in fact, his coming here has seemed to me the most ordinary thing in the world. After all, although one scarcely remembers that since the war, this is a health resort, and the man has been ill."

"Quite right," Sir Henry agreed. "You are not going to bed, dear?"

Philippa had folded up her work. She stood for a moment upon the hearth-rug. The little hardness which had tightened her mouth had disappeared, her eyes had softened.

"May I say just one word more," she begged, "about our previous—our only serious subject of conversation? I have tried my best since we were married, Henry, to make you happy."

"You know quite well," he assured her, "that you have succeeded."

"Grant me one favour, then," she pleaded. "Give up your fishing expedition to-morrow, go back to London by the first train and let me write to Lord Rayton. I am sure he would do something for you."

"Of course he'd do something!" Her husband groaned. "I should get a censorship in Ireland, or a post as instructor at Portsmouth."

"Wouldn't you rather take either of those than nothing?" she asked, "than go on living the life you are living now?"

"To be perfectly frank with you, Philippa, I wouldn't," he declared bluntly. "What on earth use should I be in a land appointment? Why, no one could read my writing, and my nautical science is entirely out of date. Why a cadet at Osborne could floor me in no time."

"You refuse to let me write, then?" she persisted.

"Absolutely."

"You intend to go on that fishing expedition with Jimmy Dumble to-morrow?"

"Wouldn't miss it for anything," he confessed.

Philippa was suddenly white with anger.

"Henry, I've finished," she declared, holding out her hand to keep him away from her. "I've finished with you entirely. I would rather be married to an enemy who was fighting honourably for his country than to you. What I have said, I mean. Don't come near me. Don't try to touch me."

She swept past him on her way to the door.

"Not even a good-night kiss?" he asked, stooping down.

She looked him in the eyes.

"I am not a child," she said scornfully.

He closed the door after her. For a moment he remained as though undecided whether to follow or not. His face had softened with her absence. Finally, however, he turned away with a little shrug of the shoulders, threw himself into his easy-chair and began to smoke furiously.

The telephone bell disturbed his reflection. He rose at once and took up the receiver.

"Yes, this is 19, Dreymarsh. Trunk call? All right, I am here."

He waited until another voice came to him faintly.

"Cranston?"

"Speaking."

"That's right. The message is Odino Berry, you understand? O-d-i-n-o b-e-r-r-y."

"I've got it," Sir Henry replied. "Good night!" He hung up the receiver, crossed the room to his desk, unlocked one of the drawers, and produced a black memorandum book, secured with a brass lock. He drew a key from his watch chain, opened the book, and ran his fingers down the O's.

"Odino," he muttered to himself. "Here it is: 'We have trustworthy information from Berlin.' Now Berry." He turned back. "'You are being watched by an enemy secret service agent.'"

He relocked the cipher book and replaced it in the desk. Then he strolled over to his easy-chair and helped himself to a whisky and soda from the tray which Mills had just arranged upon the sideboard.

"We have trustworthy information from Berlin," he repeated to himself, "that you are being watched by an enemy secret service agent."

CHAPTER VIII

"Tell me, Mr. Lessingham," Philippa insisted, "exactly what are you thinking of? You looked so dark and mysterious from the ridge below that I've climbed up on purpose to ask you."

Lessingham held out his hand to steady her. They were standing on a sharp spur of the cliffs, the north wind blowing in their faces, thrashing into little flecks of white foam the sea below, on which the twilight was already resting. For a moment or two neither of them could speak.

"I was thinking of my country," he confessed. "I was looking through the shadows there, right across the North Sea."

"To Germany?"

He shook his head.

"Further away—to Sweden."

"I forgot," she murmured. "You looked as though you were posing for a statue of some one in exile," she observed. "Come, let us go a little lower down—unless you want to stay here and be blown to pieces."

"I was on my way back to the hotel," he answered quickly, as he followed her lead, "but to tell you the truth I was feeling a little lonely."

"That," she declared, "is your own fault. I asked you to come to Mainsail Haul whenever you felt inclined."

"As I have felt inclined ever since the evening I arrived," he remarked with a smile, "you might, perhaps, by this time have had a little too much of me."

"On the contrary," she told him, "I quite expected you yesterday afternoon, to tell me how you like the place and what you have been doing. So you were thinking about—over there?" she added, moving her head seawards.

"Over there absorbs a great deal of one's thoughts," he confessed, "and the rest of them have been playing me queer tricks."

"Well, I should like to hear about the first half," she insisted.

"Do you know," he replied, "there are times when even now this war seems to me like an unreal thing, like something I have been reading about, some wild imagining of Shelley or one of the unrestrainable poets. I can't believe that millions of the flower of Germany's manhood and yours have perished helplessly, hopelessly, cruelly. And France—poor decimated France!"

"Well, Germany started the war, you know," she reminded him.

"Did she?" he answered. "I sometimes wonder. Even now I fancy, if the official papers of every one of the nations lay side by side, with their own case stated from their own point of view, even you might feel a little confused about that. Still, I am going to be very honest with you. I think myself that Germany wanted war."

"There you are, then," she declared triumphantly. "The whole thing is her responsibility."

"I do not quite go so far as that," he protested. "You see, the world is governed by great natural laws. As a snowball grows larger with rolling, so it takes up more room. As a child grows out of its infant clothes, it needs the vestments of a youth and then a man. And so with Germany. She grew and grew until the country could not hold her children, until her banks could not contain her money, until she stretched her arms out on every side and felt herself stifled. Germany came late into the world and found it parcelled out, but had she not a right to her place? She made herself great. She needed space."

"Well," Philippa observed, "you couldn't suppose that other nations were going to give up what they had, just because she wanted their possessions, could you?"

"Perhaps not," he admitted. "And yet, you see, the immutable law comes in here. The stronger must possess—not only the stronger by arms, mind, but by intellect, by learning, by proficiency in science, by utilitarianism. The really cruel part, the part I was thinking of then, as I looked out across the sea, is that this crude and miserable resort to arms should be necessary."

"If only Germans themselves were as broad-minded and reasonable as you," Philippa sighed, "one feels that there might be some hope for the future!"

"I am not alone," he assured her, "but, you see, all over Germany there is spread like a spider's web the lay religion of the citizen—devotion to the Government, blind obedience to the Kaiser. Independent thought has made Germany great in science, in political economy, in economics. But independent thought is never turned towards her political destinies. Those are shaped for her. For good or for evil her children have learnt obedience."

They were descending the hillside now. At their feet lay the little town, black and silent.

"You have helped me to understand a little," Philippa said. "You put things so gently and yet so clearly. Now tell me, will you not, how it is that you, who are a Swede by birth, are bearing arms for Germany?"

"That is very simple," he confessed. "My mother was a German, and when she died she bequeathed to me large estates in Bavaria, and a very considerable fortune. These I could never have inherited unless I had chosen to do my military service in Germany. My family is an impoverished one, and I have brothers and sisters dependent upon me. Under the circumstances, hesitation on my part was impossible."

"But when the war came?" she queried.

He looked at her in surprise.

"What was there left for me then?" he demanded. "Naturally I heard nothing but the voice of those whom I had sworn to obey. I was in that mad rush through Belgium. I was wounded at Maubeuge, or else I should have followed hard on the heels of that wonderful retreat of yours. As it was, I lay for many months in hospital. I joined again—shall I confess it?—almost unwillingly. The bloodthirstiness of it all sickened me. I fought at Ypres, but I think that it was something of the courage of despair, of black misery. I was wounded again and decorated. I suppose I shall never be fit for the front again. I tried to turn to account some of my knowledge of England and English life. Then they sent me here."

"Here, of all places in the world!" Philippa repeated wonderingly. "Just look at us! We have a single line of railway, a perfectly straightforward system of roads, the ordinary number of soldiers being trained, no mysteries, no industries—nothing. What terrible scheme are you at work upon, Mr. Lessingham?"

He smiled.

"Between you and me," he confided, "I am not at all sure that I am not here on a fool's errand—at least I thought so when I arrived."

She glanced up at him.

"And why not now?"

He made no answer, but their eyes met and Philippa looked hurriedly away. There was a moment's queer, strained silence. Before them loomed up the outline of Mainsail Haul.

"You will come in and have some tea, won't you?" she invited.

"If I may. Believe me," he added, "it has only been a certain diffidence that has kept me away so long."

She made no reply, and they entered the house together. They found Helen and Nora, with three or four young men from the Depot, having tea in the drawing-room. Lessingham slipped very easily into the pleasant little circle. If a trifle subdued, his quiet manners, and a sense of humour which every now and then displayed itself, were most attractive.

"Wish you'd come and dine with us and meet our colonel, sir," Harrison asked him. "He was at Magdalen a few years after Major Felstead, and I am sure you'd find plenty to talk about."

"I am quite sure that we should," Lessingham replied. "May I come, perhaps, towards the end of next week? I am making most strenuous efforts to lead an absolutely quiet life here."

"Whenever you like, sir. We sha'n't be able to show you anything very wild in the way of dissipation. Vintage port and a decent cigar are the only changes we can make for guests."

Philippa drew her visitor on one side presently, and made him sit with her in a distant corner of the room.

"I knew there was something I wanted to say to you," she began, "but somehow or other I forgot when I met you. My husband was very much struck with Helen's improved spirits. Don't you think that we had better tell him, when he returns, that we had heard from Major Felstead?"

Lessingham agreed.

"Just let him think that your letters came by post in the ordinary way," he advised. "I shouldn't imagine, from what I have seen of your husband, that he is a suspicious person, but it is just possible that he might have associated them with me if you had mentioned them the other night. When is he coming back?"

"I never know," Philippa answered with a sigh. "Perhaps to-night, perhaps in a week. It depends upon what sport he is having. You are not smoking."

Lessingham lit a cigarette.

"I find your husband," he said quietly, "rather an interesting type. We have no one like that in Germany. He almost puzzles me."

Philippa glanced up to find her companion's dark eyes fixed upon her.

"There is very little about Henry that need puzzle any one," she complained bitterly. "He is just an overgrown, spoilt child, devoted to amusements, and following his fancy wherever it leads him. Why do you look at me, Mr. Lessingham, as though you thought I was keeping something back? I am not, I can assure you."

"Perhaps I was wondering," he confessed, "how you really felt towards a husband whose outlook was so unnatural."

She looked down at her intertwined fingers.

"Do you know," she said softly, "I feel, somehow or other, although we have known one another such a short time, as though we were friends, and yet that is a question which I could not answer. A woman must always have some secrets, you know."

"A man may try sometimes to preserve his," he sighed, "but a woman is clever enough, as a rule, to dig them out."

A faint tinge of colour stole into her cheeks. She welcomed Helen's approach almost eagerly.

"A woman must first feel the will," she murmured, without glancing at him. "Helen, do you think we dare ask Mr. Lessingham to come and dine?"

"Please do not discourage such a delightful suggestion," Lessingham begged eagerly.

"I haven't the least idea of doing so," Helen laughed, "so long as I may have—say just ten minutes to talk about Dick."

"It is a bargain," he promised.

"We shall be quite alone," Philippa warned him, "unless Henry arrives."

"It is the great attraction of your invitation," he confessed.

"At eight o'clock, then."

CHAPTER IX

"Captain Griffiths to see your ladyship."

Philippa's fingers rested for a moment upon the keyboard of the piano before which she was seated, awaiting Lessingham's arrival. Then she glanced at the clock. It was ten minutes to eight.

"You can show him in, Mills, if he wishes to see me."

Captain Griffiths was ushered into the room—awkward, unwieldly, nervous as usual. He entered as though in a hurry, and there was nothing in his manner to denote that he had spent the last few hours making up his mind to this visit.

"I must apologise for this most untimely call, Lady Cranston," he said, watching the closing of the door. "I will not take up more than five minutes of your time."

"We are very pleased to see you at any time, Captain Griffiths," Philippa said hospitably. "Do sit down, please."

Captain Griffiths bowed but remained standing.

"It is very near your dinner-time, I know, Lady Cranston," he continued apologetically. "The fact of it is, however, that as Commandant here it is my duty to examine the bona fides of any strangers in the place. There is a gentleman named Lessingham staying at the hotel, who I understand gave your name as reference."

Philippa's eyes looked larger than ever, and her face more innocent, as she gazed up at her visitor.

"Why, of course, Captain Griffiths," she said. "Mr. Lessingham was at college with my brother, and one of his best friends. He has shot down at my father's place in Cheshire."

"You are speaking of your brother, Major Felstead?"

"My only brother."

"I am very much obliged to you, Lady Cranston," Captain Griffiths declared. "I can see that we need not worry any more about Mr. Lessingham."

Philippa laughed.

"It seems rather old-fashioned to think of you having to worry about any one down here," she observed. "It really is a very harmless neighbourhood, isn't it?"

"There isn't much going on, certainly," the Commandant admitted. "Very dull the place seems at times."

"Now be perfectly frank," Philippa begged him. "Is there a single fact of importance which could be learnt in this place, worth communicating to the enemy? Is the danger of espionage here worth a moment's consideration?"

"That," Captain Griffiths replied in somewhat stilted fashion, "is not a question which I should be prepared to answer off-hand."

Philippa shrugged her shoulders and appealed almost feverishly to Helen, who had just entered the room.

"Helen, do come and listen to Captain Griffiths! He is making me feel quite creepy. There are secrets about, it seems, and he wants to know all about Mr. Lessingham."

Helen smiled with complete self-possession.

"Well, we can set his mind at rest about Mr. Lessingham, can't we?" she observed, as she shook hands.

"We can do more," Philippa declared. "We can help him to judge for himself. We are expecting Mr. Lessingham for dinner, Captain Griffiths. Do stay."

"I couldn't think of taking you by storm like this," Captain Griffiths replied, with a wistfulness which only made his voice sound hoarser and more unpleasant. "It is most kind of you, Lady Cranston. Perhaps you will give me another opportunity."

"I sha'n't think of it," Philippa insisted. "You must stay and dine to-night. We shall be a partie carrée, for Nora goes to bed directly after dinner. I am ringing the bell to tell Mills to set an extra place," she added.

Captain Griffiths abandoned himself to fate with a little shiver of complacency. He welcomed Lessingham, who was presently announced, with very much less than his usual reserve, and the dinner was in every way a success. Towards its close, Philippa became a little thoughtful. She glanced more than once at Lessingham, who was sitting by her side, almost in admiration. His conversation, gay at times, always polished, was interlarded continually with those little social reminiscences inevitable amongst men moving in a certain circle of English society. Apparently Richard Felstead was not the only one of his college friends with whom he had kept in touch. The last remnants of Captain Griffiths' suspicions seemed to vanish with their second glass of port, although his manner became in no way more genial.

"Don't you think you are almost a little too daring?" Philippa asked her favoured guest as he helped her afterwards to set out a bridge table.

"One adapts one's methods to one's adversary," he murmured, with a smile, "Your friend Captain Griffiths had only the very conventional suspicions. The mention of a few good English names, acquaintance with the ordinary English sports, is quite sufficient with a man like that."

Helen and Griffiths were talking at the other end of the room. Philippa raised her eyes to her companion's.

"You become more of a mystery than ever," she declared. "You are making me even curious. Tell me really why you have paid us this visit from the clouds?"

She was sorry almost as soon as she had asked the question. For a moment the calm insouciance of his manner seemed to have departed. His eyes glowed.

"In search of new things," he answered.

"Guns? Fortifications?"

"Neither."

A spirit of mischief possessed her. Lessingham's manner was baffling and yet provocative. For a moment the political possibilities of his presence faded away from her mind. She had an intense desire to break through his reserve.

"Won't you tell me—why you came?"

"I could tell you more easily," he answered in a low tone, "why it will be the most miserable day of my life when I leave."

She laughed at him with perfect heartiness.

"How delightful to be flirted with again!" she sighed. "And I thought all German men were so heavy, and paid elaborate, underdone compliments. Still, your secret, sir, please? That is what I want to know."

"If you will have just a little patience!" he begged, leaning so close to her that their heads almost touched, "I promise that I will not leave this place before I tell it to you."

Philippa's eyes for the first time dropped before his. She knew perfectly well what she ought to have done and she was singularly indisposed to do it. It was a most piquant adventure, after all, and it almost helped her to forget the trouble which had been sitting so heavily in her heart. Still avoiding his eyes, she called the others.

"We are quite ready for bridge," she announced.

They played four or five rubbers. Lessingham was by far the most expert player, and he and Philippa in the end were the winners. The two men stood together for a moment or two at the sideboard, helping themselves to whisky and soda. Griffiths had become more taciturn than ever, and even Philippa was forced to admit that the latter part of the evening had scarcely been a success.

"Do you play club bridge in town, Mr. Lessingham?" Griffiths asked.

"Never," was the calm reply.

"You are head and shoulders above our class down here."

"Very good of you to say so," Lessingham replied courteously. "I held good cards to-night."

"I wonder," Griffiths went on, dropping his voice a little and keeping his eyes fixed upon his companion, "what the German substitute for bridge is."

"I wonder," Lessingham echoed.

"As a nation," his questioner proceeded, "they probably don't waste as much time on cards as we do."

Lessingham's interest in the subject appeared to be non-existent. He strolled away from the sideboard towards Philippa. She, for her part, was watching Captain Griffiths.

"So many thanks, Lady Cranston," Lessingham murmured, "for your hospitality."

"And what about that secret?" she asked.

"You see, there are two," he answered, looking down at her. "One I shall most surely tell you before I leave here, because it is the one secret which no man has ever succeeded in keeping to himself. As for the other—"

He hesitated. There was something almost like pain in his face. She broke in hastily.

"I did not call you away to ask about either. I happened to notice Captain Griffiths just now. Do you know that he is watching you very closely?"

"I had an idea of it," Lessingham admitted indifferently. "He is rather a clumsy person, is he not?"

"You will be careful?" she begged earnestly. "Remember, won't you, that Helen and I are really in a most disgraceful position if anything should come out."

"Nothing shall," he promised her. "I think you know, do you not, that, whatever might happen to me, I should find some means to protect you."

For the second time she felt a curious lack of will to fittingly reprove his boldness. She had even to struggle to keep her tone as careless as her words.

"You really are a delightful person!" she exclaimed. "How long is it since you descended from the clouds?"

"Sometimes I think that I am there still," he answered, "but I have known you about seventy-six hours."

"What precision?" she laughed. "It's a national characteristic, isn't it? Captain Griffiths," she continued, as she observed his approach, "if you really must go, please take Mr. Lessingham with you. He is making fun of me. I don't allow even Dick's friends to do that."

Lessingham's disclaimer was in quite the correct vein.

"You must both come again very soon," their hostess concluded, as she shook hands. "I enjoyed our bridge immensely."

The two men were already on their way to the door when a sudden idea seemed to occur to Captain Griffiths. He turned back.

"By-the-by, Lady Cranston," he asked, "have you heard anything from your brother?"

Philippa shook her head sadly. Helen, who, unlike her friend, had not had the advantage of a distinguished career upon the amateur dramatic stage, turned away and held a handkerchief to her eyes.

"Not a word," was Philippa's sorrowful reply.

Captain Griffiths offered a clumsy expression of his sympathy.

"Bad luck!" he said. "I'm so sorry, Lady Cranston. Good night once more."

This time their departure was uninterrupted. Helen removed her handkerchief from her eyes, and Philippa made a little grimace at the closed door.

"Do you believe," Helen asked seriously, "that Captain Griffiths has any suspicions?"

Philippa shrugged her shoulders.

"If he has, who cares?" she replied, a little defiantly. "The very idea of a duel of wits between those two men is laughable."

"Perhaps so," Helen agreed, with a shade of doubt in her tone.

CHAPTER X

Philippa and Helen started, a few mornings later, for one of their customary walks. The crystalline October sunshine, in which every distant tree and, seaward, each slowly travelling steamer, seemed to gain a new clearness of outline, lay upon the deep-ploughed fields, the yellowing bracken, and the red-gold of the bending trees, while the west wind, which had strewn the sea with white-flecked waves, brought down the leaves to form a carpet for their feet, and played strange music along the wood-crested slope. In the broken land through which they made their way, a land of trees and moorland, with here and there a cultivated patch, the yellow gorse still glowed in unexpected corners; queer, scentless flowers made splashes of colour in the hedgerows; a rabbit scurried sometimes across their path; a cock pheasant, after a moment's amazed stare, lowered his head and rushed for unnecessary shelter. The longer they looked upwards, the bluer seemed the sky. The grass beneath their feet was as green and soft as in springtime. Driven by the wind, here and there a white-winged gull sailed over their heads,—a cloud of them rested upon a freshly turned little square of ploughed land between two woods. A flight of pigeons, like torn leaves tossed about by the wind, circled and drifted above them. Philippa seated herself upon the trunk of a fallen tree and gazed contentedly about her.

"If I had a looking-glass and a few more hairpins, I should be perfectly happy," she sighed. "I am sure my hair must look awful."

Helen glanced at it admiringly.

"I decline to say the correct thing," she declared. "I will only remind you that there will be no one here to look at it."

"I am not so sure," Philippa replied. "These are the woods which the special constables haunt by day and by night. They gaze up every tree trunk for a wireless installation, and they lie behind hedges and watch for mysterious flashes."

"Are you suggesting that we may meet Mr. Lessingham?" Helen enquired, lazily. "I am perfectly certain that he knows nothing of the equipment of the melodramatic spy. As to Zeppelins, don't you remember he told us that he hated them and was terrified of bombs."

"My dear," Philippa remonstrated, "Mr. Lessingham does nothing crude."

"And yet,—" Helen began.

"Yet I suppose the man has something at the back of his head," Philippa interrupted. "Sometimes I think that he has, sometimes I believe that Richard must have shown him my picture, and he has come over here to see if I am really like it."

"He does behave rather like that," her companion admitted drily.

Phillipa turned and looked at her.

"Helen," she said severely, "don't be a cat."

"If I were to express my opinion of your behaviour," Helen went on, picking up a pine cone and examining it, "I might astonish you."

"You have an evil mind," Philippa yawned, producing her cigarette case. "What you really resent is that Mr. Lessingham sometimes forgets to talk about Dick."

"The poor man doesn't get much chance," Helen retorted, watching the blue smoke from her cigarette and leaning back with an air of content. "Whatever do you and he find to talk about, Philippa?"

"Literature—English and German," Philippa murmured demurely. "Mr. Lessingham is remarkably well read, and he knows more about our English poets than any man I have met for years."

"I forgot that you enjoyed that sort of thing."

"Once more, don't be a cat," Philippa enjoined. "If you want me to confess it, I will own up at once. You know what a simple little thing I am. I admire Mr. Lessingham exceedingly, and I find him a most interesting companion."

"You mean," her friend observed drily "the Baron Maderstrom." Philippa looked around and frowned.

"You are most indiscreet, Helen," she declared. "I have learnt something of the science of espionage lately, and I can assure you that all spoken or written words are dangerous. There is a thoroughly British squirrel in that tree overhead, and I am sure he heard."

"I suppose the sunshine has got into your head," Helen groaned.

"If you mean that I am finding it a relief to talk nonsense, you are right," Philippa assented. "As a matter of fact, I am feeling most depressed. Henry telephoned from somewhere or other before breakfast this morning, to say that he should probably be home to-night or to-morrow. They must have landed somewhere down the coast."

"You are a most undutiful wife," Helen pronounced severely. "I am sure Henry is a delightful person, even if he is a little irresponsible, and it is almost pathetic to remember how much you were in love with him, a year or two ago."

Some of the lightness vanished from Philippa's face.

"That was before the war," she sighed.

"I still think Henry is a dear, though I don't altogether understand him," Helen said thoughtfully.

"No doubt," Philippa assented, "but you'd find the not understanding him a little more galling, if you were his wife. You see, I didn't know that I was marrying a sort of sporting Mr. Skimpole."

"I wonder," Helen reflected, "how Henry and Mr. Lessingham will get on when they see more of one another."

"I really don't care," Philippa observed indifferently.

"I used to notice sometimes—that was soon after you were married," Helen continued, "that Henry was just a little inclined to be jealous."

Philippa withdrew her eyes from the sea. There was a queer little smile upon her lips.

"Well, if he still is," she said, "I'll give him something to be jealous about."

"Poor Mr. Lessingham!" Helen murmured.

Philippa's eyebrows were raised.

"Poor Mr. Lessingham?" she repeated. "I don't think you'll find that he'll be in the least sorry for himself."

"He may be in earnest," Helen reminded her friend. "You can be horribly attractive when you like, you know, Philippa."

Philippa smiled sweetly.

"It is just possible," she said, "that I may be in earnest myself. I've quarrelled pretty desperately with Henry, you know, and I'm a helpless creature without a little admiration."

Helen rose suddenly to her feet. Her eyes were fixed upon a figure approaching through the wood.

"You really aren't respectable, Philippa," she declared. "Throw away your cigarette, for heaven's sake, and sit up. Some one is coming."

Philippa only moved her head lazily. The sunlight, which came down in a thousand little zigzags through the wind-tossed trees, fell straight upon her rather pale, defiant little face, with its unexpressed evasive charm, and seemed to find a new depth of colour in the red-gold of her disordered hair. Her slim, perfect body was stretched almost at full length, one leg drawn a little up, her hands carelessly drooping towards the grass. The cigarette was still burning in the corner of her lips.

"I decline," she said, "to throw away my cigarette for any one."

"Least of all, I trust," a familiar voice interposed, "for me."

Philippa sat upright at once, smoothed her hair and looked a little resentfully at Lessingham. He was wearing a brown tweed knickerbocker suit, and he carried a gun under his arm.

"Whatever are you doing up here," she demanded, "and do you know anything about our game laws? You can't come out into the woods here and shoot things just because you feel like it."

He disposed of his gun and seated himself between them.

"That is quite all right," he assured her. "Your neighbour, Mr. Windover, to whom these woods apparently belong, asked me to bring my gun out this morning and try and get a woodcock."

"Gracious! You don't mean that Mr. Windover is here, too?" Philippa demanded, looking around. Lessingham shook his head.

"His car came for him at the other side of the wood," he explained. "He was wanted to go on the Bench. I elected to walk home."

"And the woodcock?" she asked. "I adore woodcock."

He produced one from his pocket, took up her felt hat, which was lying amongst the bracken, and busied himself insinuating the pin feathers under the silk band.

"There," he said, handing it to her, "the first woodcock of the season. We got four, and I really only accepted one in the hope that you would like it. I shall leave it with the estimable Mills, on my return."

"You must come and share it," Philippa insisted. "Those boys of Nora's are coming in to dinner. Your gift shall be the piece de resistance."

"Then may I dine another night?" he begged. "This place encourages in me the grossest of appetites."

"Have no fear," she replied. "You will never see that woodcock again. I shall have it for my luncheon to-morrow. I ordered dinner before I came out, and though it may be a simple feast, I promise that you shall not go away hungry."

"Will you promise that you will never send me away hungry?" he asked, dropping his voice for a moment.

She turned and studied him. Helen, who had strolled a few yards away, was knee-deep in the golden brown bracken, picking some gorgeously coloured leaves from a solitary bramble bush. Lessingham had thrown his cap onto the ground, and his wind-tossed hair and the unusual colour in his cheeks were both, in their way, becoming. His loose but well-fitting country clothes, his tie and soft collar, were all well-chosen and suitable. She admired his high forehead and his firm, rather proud mouth. His eyes as well as his tone were full of seriousness.

"You know that you ought to be saying that to some Gretchen away across that terrible North Sea," she laughed.

"There is no Gretchen who has ever made my heart shake as you do," he whispered.

She picked up her hat and sighed.

"Really," she said, "I think things are quite complicated enough as they are. I am in a flutter all day long, as it is, about your mission here and your real identity. I simply could not include a flirtation amongst my excitements."

"I have never flirted," he assured her gravely.

"Wise man," she pronounced, rising to her feet. "Come, let us go and help Helen pick leaves. She is scratching her fingers terribly, and I'm sure you have a knife. A dear, economical creature, Helen," she added, as they strolled along. "I am perfectly certain that those are destined to adorn my dining-table, and, with chrysanthemums at sixpence each, you can't imagine how welcome they are. Come, produce the knife, Mr. Lessingham."

The knife was forthcoming, and presently they all turned their faces homeward. Philippa arrested both her companions on the outskirts of the wood, and pointed to the red-tiled little town, to the sombre, storm-beaten grey church on the edge of the cliff, to the peaceful fields, the stretch of gorse-sprinkled common, and the rolling stretch of green turf on the crown of the cliffs. Beyond was the foam-flecked blue sea, dotted all over with cargo steamers.

"Would one believe," she asked satirically, "that there should be scope here in this forgotten little spot for the brains of a—Mr. Lessingham!"

"Remember that I was sent," he protested. "The error, if error there be, is not mine."

"And after all," Helen reminded them both, "think how easily one may be misled by appearances. You couldn't imagine anything more honest than the faces of the villagers and the fishermen one sees about, yet do you know, Mr. Lessingham, that we were visited by burglars last night?"

"Seriously?" he asked.

"Without a doubt. Of course, Mainsail Haul is an invitation to thieves. They could get in anywhere. Last night they chose the French windows and seem to have made themselves at home in the library."

"I trust," Lessingham said, "that they did not take anything of value?"

"They took nothing at all," Philippa sighed. "That is the humiliating part of it. They evidently didn't like our things."

"How do you know that you had burglars, if they took nothing away?" Lessingham enquired.

"So practical!" Philippa murmured. "As a matter of fact, I heard some one moving about, and I rang the alarm bell. Mills was downstairs almost directly and we heard some one running down the drive. The French windows were open, a chair was overturned in the library, and a drawer in my husband's desk was wide open."

"The proof," Lessingham admitted, "is overwhelming. You were visited by a burglar. Does your husband keep anything of value in his desk?"

"Henry hasn't anything of value in the world," Philippa replied drily, "except his securities, and they are at the bank."

"Without going so far as to contradict you," Lessingham observed, with a smile, "I still venture to disagree!"

CHAPTER XI

Sir Henry stepped back from the scales and eyed the fish which they had been weighing, admiringly.

"You see that, Mills? You see that, Jimmy?" he pointed out. "Six and three-quarter pounds! I was right almost to an ounce. He's a fine fellow!"

"A very extraordinary fish, sir," the butler observed. "Will you allow me to take your oilskins? Dinner was served nearly an hour ago."

Sir Henry slipped off his dripping overalls and handed them over.

"That's all right," he replied. "Listen. Don't say a word about my arrival to your mistress at present. I have some writing to do. Bring me a glass of sherry at once, or mix a cocktail if you can do so without being missed, and take Jimmy away and give him some whisky and soda."

"But what about your own dinner, sir?"

"I'll have a tray in the gun room," his master decided, "say in twenty minutes' time. And, Mills, who did you say were dining?"

"Two of the young officers from the Depot, sir—Mr. Harrison and Mr. Sinclair—and Mr. Hamar Lessingham."

"Lessingham, eh?" Sir Henry repeated, as he seated himself before his writing-table. "Mills," he added, in a confidential whisper, "what port did you serve?"

The butler's expression was one of conscious rectitude.

"Not the vintage, sir," he announced with emphasis. "Some very excellent wood port, which we procured for shooting luncheons. The young gentlemen like it."

"You're a jewel, Mills," his master declared. "Now you understand—an aperitif for me now, some whisky for Jimmy in your room, and not a word about my being here. Good night, Jimmy. Sorry we were too late for the mackerel, but we had some grand sport, all the same. You'll have a day or two's rest ashore now."

"Aye, aye, sir!" Dumble replied. "We got in just in time. There's something more than a squall coming up nor'ards."

Sir Henry listened for a moment. The French windows shook, the rain beat against the panes, and a dull booming of wind was clearly audible from outside.

"We timed that excellently," he agreed. "Come up and have a chat to-morrow, Jimmy, if your wife will spare you."

"I'll be round before eleven, sir," the fisherman promised, with a grin.

Sir Henry waited for the closing of the door. Then he leaned forward for several moments. He had scarcely the appearance of a man returned from a week or two of open-air life and indulgence in the sport he loved best. The healthy tan of his complexion was lessened rather than increased. There were black lines under his eyes which seemed to speak of sleepless nights, and a beard of several days' growth was upon his chin. He drank the cocktail which Mills presently brought him, at a gulp, and watched with satisfaction while the mixer was vigorously shaken and a second one poured out.

"We've had a rough time, Mills," he observed, as he set down the glass. "Until this morning it scarcely left off blowing."

"I'm sorry to hear it, sir," was the respectful reply. "If I may be allowed to say so, sir, you're looking tired."

"I am tired," Sir Henry admitted. "I think, if I tried, I could go to sleep now for twenty-four hours."

"You will pardon my reminding you, so far as regards your letters, that there is no post out tonight, sir," Mills proceeded. "I have prepared a warm bath and laid out your clothes for a change."

"Capital!" Sir Henry exclaimed. "It isn't a letter that's bothering me, though, Mills. There are just a few geographical notes I want to make. You know, I'm trying to improve the fishermen's chart of the coast round here. That fellow Groocock—Jimmy Dumble's uncle—very nearly lost his motor boat last week through trusting to the old one."

"Just so, sir," Mills replied deferentially, placing the empty glass upon his tray. "If you'll excuse me, sir, I must get back to the dining room."

"Quite right," his master assented. "They won't be out just yet, will they?"

"Her ladyship will probably be rising in about ten minutes, sir—not before that."

Sir Henry nodded a little impatiently. Directly the door was closed he rose to his feet, stood for a moment listening by the side of his fishing cabinet, then opened the glass front and touched the spring. With the aid of a little electric torch which he took from his pocket, he studied particularly a certain portion of the giant chart, made some measurements with a pencil, some notes in the margin, and closed it up again with an air of satisfaction. Then he resumed his seat, drew a folded slip of paper from his breast pocket, a chart from another, turned up the lamp and began to write. His face, as he stooped low, escaped the soft shade and was for a moment almost ghastly. Every now and then he turned and made some calculations on the blotting-paper by his side. At last he leaned back with a little sigh of relief. He had barely done so before the door behind him was opened.

"Are we going to stay in here, Mummy, or are we going into the drawing-room?" Nora asked.

"In here, I think," he heard Philippa reply.

Then they both came in, followed by Helen. Nora was the first to see him and rushed forward with a little cry of surprise.

"Why, here's Dad!" she exclaimed, flinging her arms around his neck. "Daddy, how dare you be sitting here all by yourself whilst we are having dinner! When did you get back? What a fish!"

Sir Henry closed down his desk, embraced his daughter, and came forward to meet his wife.

"Fine fellow, isn't he, Nora!" he agreed. "Well, Philippa, how are you? Pleased to see me, I hope? Another new frock, I believe, and in war time!"

"Fancy your remembering that it was war time!" she answered, standing very still while he leaned over and kissed her.

"Nasty one for me," Sir Henry observed good-humouredly. "How well you're looking, Helen! Any news of Dick yet?"

Helen attempted an expression of extreme gravity with more or less success.

"Nothing fresh," she answered.

"Well, well, no news may be good news," Sir Henry remarked consolingly. "Jove, it's good to feel a roof over one's head again! This morning has been the only patch of decent weather we've had."

"This morning was lovely," Helen assented. "Philippa and I went and sat up in the woods."

Philippa, who was standing by the fire, turned and looked at her husband critically.

"We have some men dining," she said. "They will be out in a few minutes. Don't you think you had better go and make yourself presentable? You smell of fish, and you look as though you hadn't shaved for a week."

"Guilty, my dear," Sir Henry admitted. "Mills is just getting me something to eat in the gun room, and then I am going to have a bath and change my clothes."

"And shave, Dad," Nora reminded him.

"And shave, you young pest," her father agreed, patting her on the shoulder. "Run away and play billiards with Helen. I want to talk to your mother until my dinner's ready."

Nora acquiesced promptly.

"Come along, Helen, I'll give you twenty-five up. Or perhaps you'd like to play shell out?" she proposed. "Arthur Sinclair says I have improved in my potting more than any one he ever knew."

Sir Henry opened the door and closed it after them. Then he returned and seated himself on the lounge by Philippa's side. She glanced up at him as though in surprise, and, stretching out her hand towards her work-basket, took up some knitting.

"I really think I should change at once, if I were you," she suggested.

"Presently. I had a sort of foolish idea that I'd like to have a word or two with you first. I've been away for nearly a fortnight, haven't I?"

"You have," Philippa assented. "Perhaps that is the reason why I feel that I haven't very much to say to you."

"That sounds just a trifle hard," he said slowly.

"I am hard sometimes," Philippa confessed. "You know that quite well. There are times when I just feel as though I had no heart at all, nor any sympathy; when every sensation I might have had seems shrivelled up inside me."

"Is that how you are feeling at the present time towards me, Philippa?" he asked.

Her needles flashed through the wool for a moment in silence.

"You had every warning," she told him. "I tried to make you understand exactly how your behaviour disgusted me before you went away."

"Yes, I remember," he admitted. "I'm afraid, dear, you think I am a worthless sort of a fellow."

Philippa had apparently dropped a stitch. She bent lower still over her knitting. There was a distinct frown upon her forehead, her mouth was unrecognisable.

"Your friend Lessingham is here still, I understand?" her husband remarked presently.

"Yes," Philippa assented, "he is dining to-night. You will probably see him in a few minutes."

Sir Henry looked thoughtful, and studied for a moment the toe of a remarkably unprepossessing looking shoe.

"You're so keen about that sort of thing," he said, "what about Lessingham? He is not soldiering or anything, is he?"

"I have no idea," Philippa replied. "He walks with a slight limp and admits that he is here as a convalescent, but he hasn't told us very much about himself."

"I wonder you haven't tackled him," Sir Henry continued. "You're such an ardent recruiter, you ought to make sure that he is doing his bit of butchery."

Philippa looked up at her husband for a moment and back at her work.

"Mr. Lessingham," she said, "is a very delightful friend, whose stay here every one is enjoying very much, but he is a comparative stranger. I feel no responsibility as to his actions."

"And you do as to mine?"

"Naturally."

Sir Henry's head was resting on his hand, his elbow on the back of the lounge. He seemed to be listening to the voices in the dining room beyond.

"Hm!" he observed. "Has he been here often while I've been away?"

"As often as he chose," Philippa replied. "He has become very popular in the neighbourhood already, and he is an exceedingly welcome guest here at any time."

"Takes advantage of your hospitality pretty often, doesn't he?"

"He is here most days. We are always rather disappointed when he doesn't come."

Sir Henry's frown grew a little deeper.

"What's the attraction?" he demanded.

Philippa smiled. It was the smile which those who knew her best, feared.

"Well," she confided, "I used to imagine that it was Helen, but I think that he has become a little bored, talking about nothing but Dick and their college days. I am rather inclined to fancy that it must be me."

"You, indeed!" he grunted. "Are you aware that you are a married woman?"

Philippa glanced up from her work. Her eyebrows were raised, and her expression was one of mild surprise.

"How queer that you should remind me of it!" she murmured. "I am afraid that the sea air disturbs your memory."

Sir Henry rose abruptly to his feet.

"Oh, damn!" he exclaimed.

He walked to the door. His guests were still lingering over their wine. He could hear their voices more distinctly than ever. Then he came back to the sofa and stood by Philippa's side.

"Philippa, old girl," he pleaded, "don't let us quarrel. I have had such a hard fortnight, a nor'easter blowing all the time, and the dirtiest seas I've ever known at this time of the year. For five days I hadn't a dry stitch on me, and it was touch and go more than once. We were all in the water together, and there was a nasty green wave that looked like a mountain overhead, and the side of our own boat bending over us as though it meant to squeeze our ribs in. It looked like ten to one against us, Phil, and I got a worse chill than the sea ever gave me when I thought that I shouldn't see you again."

Philippa laid down her knitting. She looked searchingly into her husband's face. She was very far from indifferent to his altered tone.

"Henry," she said, "that sounds very terrible, but why do you run such risks—unworthily? Do you think that I couldn't give you all that you want, all that I have to give, if you came home to me with a story like this and I knew that you had been facing death righteously and honourably for your country's sake? Why, Henry, there isn't a man in the world could have such a welcome as I could give you. Do you think I am cold? Of course you don't! Do you think I want to feel as I have done this last fortnight towards you? Why, it's misery! It makes me feel inclined to commit any folly, any madness, to get rid of it all."

Her husband hesitated. A frown had darkened his face. He had the air of one who is on the eve of a confession.

"Philippa," he began, "you know that when I go out on these fishing expeditions, I also put in some work at the new chart which I am so anxious to prepare for the fishermen."

Philippa shook her head impatiently.

"Don't talk to me about your fishermen, Henry! I'm as sick with them as I am with you. You can see twenty or thirty of them any morning, lounging about the quay, strapping young fellows who shelter themselves behind the plea of privileged employment. We are notorious down here for our skulkers, and you—you who should be the one man to set them an example, are as bad as they are. You deliberately encourage them."

Sir Henry abandoned his position by his wife's side, His face darkened and his eyes flashed.

"Skulkers?" he repeated furiously.

Philippa looked at him without flinching.

"Yes! Don't you like the word?"

The angry flush faded from his cheeks as quickly as it had come. He laughed a little unnaturally, took up a cigarette from an open box, and lit it.

"It isn't a pleasant one, is it, Philippa?" he observed, thrusting his hands into his jacket pockets strolling away. "If one doesn't feel the call—well, there you are, you see. Jove, that's a fine fish."

He stood admiring the codling upon the scales. Philippa continued her work.

"If you intend to spend the rest of the evening with us," she told him calmly, "please let me remind you again that we have guests for dinner. Your present attire may be comfortable but it is scarcely becoming."

He turned away and came back towards her. As he passed the lamp, she started.

"Why, you're wet," she exclaimed, "wet through!"

"Of course I am," he admitted, feeling his sleeve, "but to tell you the truth, in the interest of our conversation I had quite forgotten it. Here come our guests, before I have had time to escape. I can hear your friend Lessingham's voice."

CHAPTER XII

The three dinner guests entered together, Lessingham in the middle. Sir Henry's presence was obviously a surprise to all of them.

"No idea that you were back, sir," Harrison observed, shaking hands.

Sir Henry greeted them all good-humouredly. "I turned up about three quarters of an hour ago," he explained, "just too late to join you at dinner."

"Bad luck, sir," Sinclair remarked. "I hope that you had good sport?"

"Not so bad," Sir Henry admitted. "We had to go far enough for it, though. What do you think of that for an October codling?"

They all approached the scales and admired the fish. Sir Henry stood with his hands in his pockets, listening to their comments.

"You are enjoying your stay here, I hope, Mr. Lessingham?" he enquired.

"One could scarcely fail to enjoy even the briefest holiday in so delightfully hospitable a place," was the somewhat measured reply.

"You're by way of being a fisherman yourself, I hear?" Sir Henry continued.

"In a very small way," Lessingham acknowledged. "I have been out once or twice."

"With Ben Oates, eh?"

"I believe that was the man's name."

Philippa glanced up from her work with a little exclamation of surprise.

"I had no idea of that, Mr. Lessingham. Whatever made you choose Ben Oates? He is a most disgraceful person."

"It was entirely by accident," Lessingham explained. "I met him on the front. It happened to be a fine morning, and he was rather pressing in his invitation."

"I'm afraid he didn't show you much sport," Sir Henry observed. "From what Jimmy Dumble's brother told him, he seems to have taken you in entirely the wrong direction, and on the wrong tide."

"We had a small catch," Lessingham replied. "I really went more for the sail than the sport, so I was not disappointed."

"The coast itself," Sir Henry remarked, "is rather an interesting one."

"I should imagine so," Lessingham assented. "Mr. Ben Oates, indeed, told me some wonderful stories about it. He spoke of broad channels down which a dreadnought could approach within a hundred yards of the land."

"He is quite right, too," his host agreed.

"There's a lot of deep water about here. The whole of the coast is very curious in that way. What the—what the dickens is this?"

Sir Henry, who had been strolling about the room, picked up a Homburg hat from the far side of a table of curios. Philippa glanced up at his exclamation.

"That's Nora's trophy," she explained. "I told her to take it up to her own room, but she's always wanting to show it to her friends."

"Nora's trophy?" Sir Henry repeated. "Why, it's nothing but an ordinary man's hat."

"Nevertheless, it's a very travelled one, sir," Harrison pointed out. "Miss Nora picked it up on Dutchman's Common, the morning after the observation car was found there."

Sir Henry held out the hat.

"But Nora doesn't seriously suppose that the Germans come over in this sort of headgear, does she?" he demanded.

"If you'll just look inside the lining, sir," Sinclair suggested.

Sir Henry turned it up and whistled softly. "By Jove, it's a German hat, all right!" he exclaimed. "Doesn't look a bad shape, either."

He tried it on. There was a little peal of laughter from the men. Philippa had ceased her knitting and was watching from the couch. Sir Henry looked at himself in the looking-glass.

"Well, that's funny," he observed. "I shouldn't have thought it would have been so much too small for me. Here, just try how you'd look in it, Mr. Lessingham," he added, handing it across to him.

Lessingham accepted the situation quite coolly, and placed the hat carefully on his head.

"It doesn't feel particularly comfortable," he remarked.

"That may be," Sir Henry suggested, "because you have it on wrong side foremost. If you'd just turn it round, I believe you would find it a very good fit."

Lessingham at once obeyed. Sir Henry regarded him with admiration.

"Excellent!" he exclaimed. "Look at that, Philippa. Might have been made for him, eh?"

Lessingham looked at himself in the glass and removed the hat from his head with some casual observation. He was entirely at his ease. His host turned towards the door, which Mills was holding open.

"Captain Griffiths, sir," the latter announced.

Sir Henry greeted his visitor briefly.

"How are you, Griffiths?" he said. "Glad to see you. Excuse my costume, but I am just back from a fishing expedition. We are all admiring Mr. Lessingham in his magic hat."

Captain Griffiths shook hands with Philippa, nodded to the others, and turned towards Lessingham.

"Put it on again, there's a good fellow, Lessingham," Sir Henry begged. "You see, we have found a modern version of Cinderella's slipper. The hat which fell from the Zeppelin on to Dutchman's Common fits our friend like a glove. I never thought the Germans made such good hats, did you, Griffiths?"

"I always thought they imported their felt hats," Captain Griffiths acknowledged. "Is that really the one with the German name inside, which Miss Nora brought home?"

"This is the genuine article," Lessingham assented, taking it from his head and passing it on to the newcomer. "Notwithstanding the name inside, I should still believe that it was an English hat. It feels too comfortable for anything else."

The Commandant took the hat to a lamp and examined it carefully. He drew out the lining and looked all the way round. Suddenly he gave vent to a little exclamation.

"Here are the owner's initials," he declared, "rather faint but still distinguishable,—B. M. Hm! There's no doubt about its being a German hat."

"B. M.," Sir Henry muttered, looking over his shoulder. "How very interesting! B. M.," he repeated, turning to Philippa, who had recommenced her knitting. "Is it my fancy, or is there something a little familiar about that?"

"I am sure that I have no idea," Philippa replied. "It conveys nothing to me."

There was a brief but apparently pointless silence. Philippa's needles flashed through her wool with easy regularity. Lessingham appeared to be sharing the mild curiosity which the others showed concerning the hat. Sir Henry was standing with knitted brows, in the obvious attitude of a man seeking to remember something.

"B. M.," he murmured softly to himself. "There was some one I've known or heard of in England—What's that, Mills?"

"Your dinner is served, sir," Mills, who had made a silent entrance, announced.

Sir Henry apparently thought no more of the hat or its possible owner. He threw it upon a neighbouring table, and his face expressed a new interest in life.

"Jove, I'm ravenous!" he confessed. "You'll excuse me, won't you? Mills, see that these gentlemen have cigars and cigarettes—in the billiard room, I should think. You'll find the young people there. I'll come in and have a game of pills later."

The two young soldiers, with Captain Griffiths, followed Sir Henry at once from the room. Lessingham, however, lingered. He stood with his hands behind him, looking at the closed door.

"Are you going to stay and talk nonsense with me, Mr. Lessingham?" Philippa asked.

"If I may," he answered, without changing his position.

Philippa looked at him curiously.

"Do you see ghosts through that door?"

He shook his head.

"Do you know," he said, as he seated himself by her side, "there are times when I find your husband quite interesting."

CHAPTER XIII

Philippa leaned back in her place.

"Exactly what do you mean by that, Mr. Lessingham?" she demanded.

He shook himself free from a curious sense of unreality, and turned towards her.

"I must confess," he said, "that sometimes your husband puzzles me."

"Not nearly so much as he puzzles me," Philippa retorted, a little bitterly.

"Has he always been so desperately interested in deep-sea fishing?"

Philippa shrugged her shoulders.

"More or less, but never quite to this extent. The thing has become an obsession with him lately. If you are really going to stay and talk with me, do you mind if we don't discuss my husband? Just now the subject is rather a painful one with me."

"I can quite understand that," Lessingham murmured sympathetically.

"What do you think of Captain Griffiths?" she asked, a little abruptly.

"I have thought nothing more about him. Should I? Is he of any real importance?"

"He is military commandant here."

Lessingham nodded thoughtfully.

"I suppose that means that he is the man who ought to be on my track," he observed.

"I shouldn't be in the least surprised to hear that he was," Philippa said drily. "I have told you that he came and asked about you the other night, when he dined here. He seemed perfectly satisfied then, but he is here again to-night to see Henry, and he never visits anywhere in an ordinary way."

"Are you uneasy about me?" Lessingham enquired.

"I am not sure," she answered frankly. "Sometimes I am almost terrified and would give anything to hear that you were on your way home. And at other times I realise that you are really very clever, that nothing is likely to happen to you, and that the place will seem duller than ever when you do go."

"That is very kind of you," he said. "In any case, I fear that my holiday will soon be coming to an end."

"Your holiday?" she repeated. "Is that what you call it?"

"It has been little else," he replied indifferently. "There is nothing to be learnt here of the slightest military significance."

"We told you that when you arrived," Philippa reminded him.

"I was perhaps foolish not to believe you," he acknowledged.

"So your very exciting journey through the clouds has ended in failure, after all!" she went on, a moment or two later.

"Failure? No, I should not call it failure."

"You have really made some discoveries, then?" she enquired dubiously.

"I have made the greatest discovery in the world."

Her eyebrows were gently raised, the corners of her mouth quivered, her eyes fell.

"Dear me! In this quiet spot?" she sighed.

"Yes!"

"Is it Helen or me?"

"Philippa!" he protested.

Her eyebrows were more raised than ever. Her mouth had lost its alluring curve.

"Really, Mr. Lessingham!" she exclaimed. "Have I ever given you the right to call me by my Christian name?"

"In my country," he answered, "we do not wait to ask. We take."

"Rank Prussianism," she murmured. "I really think you had better go back there. You are adopting their methods."

"I may have to at any moment," he admitted, "or to some more distant country still. I want something to take back with me."

"You want a keepsake, of course," Philippa declared, looking around the room. "You can have my photograph—the one over there. Helen will give you one of hers, too, I am sure, if you ask her. She is just as grateful to you about Richard as I am."

"But from you," he said earnestly, "I want more than gratitude."

"Dear me, how persistent you are!" Philippa murmured. "Are you really determined to make love to me?"

"Ah, don't mock me!" he begged. "What I am saying to you comes from my heart."

Philippa laughed at him quietly. There was just a little break in her voice, however.

"Don't be absurd!"

"There is nothing absurd about it," he replied, with a note of sadness in his tone. "I felt it from the moment we met. I struggled against it, but I have felt it growing day by day. I came here with my mind filled with different purposes. I had no thought of amusing myself, no thought of seeking here the happiness which up till now I seem to have missed. I came as a servant because I was sent, a mechanical being. You have changed everything. For you I feel what I have never felt for any woman before. I place before you my career, my freedom, my honour."

Philippa sighed very softly.

"Do you mind ringing the bell?" she begged.

"The bell?" he repeated. "What for?"

"I want Helen to hear you," she confided, with a wonderful little smile.

"Philippa, don't mock me," he pleaded. "If this is only amusement to you, tell me so and let me go away. It is the first time in my life that a woman has come between me and my work. I am no longer master of myself. I am obsessed with you. I want nothing else in life but your love."

There was an almost startling change in Philippa's face. The banter which had served her with so much effect, which she had relied upon as her defensive weapon, was suddenly useless. Lessingham had created an atmosphere around him, an atmosphere of sincerity.

"Are you in earnest?" she faltered.

"God knows I am!" he insisted.

"You—you care for me?"

"So much," he answered passionately, "that for your sake I would sacrifice my honour, my country, my life."

"But I've only known you for such a short time," Philippa protested, "and you're an enemy."

"I discard my birth. I renounce my adopted country," he declared fiercely. "You have swept my life clear of every scrap of ambition and patriotism. You have filled it with one thing only—a great, consuming love."

"Have you forgotten my husband?"

"Do you think that if he had been a different sort of man I should have dared to speak? Ask yourself how you can continue to live with him? You can call him which you will. Both are equally disgraceful. Your heart knows the truth. He is either a coward or a philanderer."

Philippa's cheeks were suddenly white. Her eyes flashed. His words had stung her to the quick.

"A coward?" she repeated furiously. "You dare to call Henry that?"

Lessingham rose abruptly to his feet. He moved restlessly about the room. His fists were clenched, his tone thick with passion.

"I do!" he pronounced. "Philippa, look at this matter without prejudice. Do you believe that there is a single man of any country, of your husband's age and rank, who would be content to trawl the seas for fish whilst his country's blood is being drained dry? Who would weigh a codling," he added, pointing scornfully to the scales, "whilst the funeral march of heroes is beating throughout the world? The thing is insensate, impossible!"

Philippa's head drooped. Her hands were nervously intertwined.

"Don't!" she pleaded, "I have suffered so much."

"Forgive me," he begged, with a sudden change of voice. "If I am mistaken in your husband—and there is always the chance—I am sorry. I will confess that I myself had a different opinion of him, but I can only judge from what I have seen and from that there is no one in the world who would not agree with me that your husband is unworthy of you."

"Oh, please stop!" Philippa cried. "Stop at once!"

Lessingham came back to his place by her side. His voice was still shaking, but it had grown very soft.

"Philippa, forgive me," he repeated. "If you only knew how it hurts to see you like this! Yet I must speak. There is just once in every man's lifetime when he must tell the truth. That time has come with me—I love you."

"So does my husband," she murmured.

"I will only remind you, then, that he shows it in strange fashion," Lessingham continued. "He sets your wishes at defiance. He who should be an example in a small place like this, is only an object of contempt in the neighbourhood. Even I, who have only lived here for so short a time, have caught the burden of what people say."

Philippa wiped her eyes.

"Please, do you mind," she begged, "not saying anything more about Henry. You are only reminding me of things which I try all the time to forget."

"Believe me," Lessingham answered wistfully, "I am only too content to ignore him, to forget that he exists, to remember only that you are the woman who has changed my life."

Philippa looked at him in something like dismay, rather like a child who has started an engine which she has no idea how to stop.

"But you must not—you must not talk to me like this!"

His hand closed upon hers. It lay in his grasp, unyielding, cold, yet passive.

"Why not?" he whispered. "I have the one unalterable right, and I am willing to pay the great price."

"Right?" she faltered.

"The right of loving you—the right of loving you better than any woman in the world."

There was a queer silence, only partly due, as she was instantly aware, to the emotion of the moment. A door behind them had opened. Philippa's quicker senses had recognised her husband's footsteps. Lessingham rose deliberately to his feet. In his heart he welcomed the interruption. This might, perhaps, be the decisive moment. Sir Henry was strolling towards them. His manner and his tone, however, were alike good-natured.

"I was to order you into the billiard room, Mr. Lessingham," he announced. "Sinclair has been sent for—a night route march, or some such horror—and they want you to make a four."

Lessingham hesitated. He had a passionate inclination to face the situation, to tell this man the truth. Sir Henry's courteous indifference, however, was like a harrier. He recognised the inevitable.

"I am afraid I am rather out of practice," he said, "but I shall be delighted to do my best."

CHAPTER XIV

Sir Henry was obviously not in the best of tempers. For a mild-mannered and easy-going man, his expression was scarcely normal.

"That fellow was making love to you," he said bluntly, as soon as the door was closed behind Lessingham.

Philippa looked up at her husband with an air of pleasant candour.

"He was doing it very nicely, too," she admitted.

"You mean to say that you let him?"

"I listened to what he had to say," she confessed. "It didn't occur to you, I suppose," her husband remarked, with somewhat strained sarcasm, "that you were another man's wife?"

"I am doing my best to forget that fact," Philippa reminded him.

"I see! And he is to help you?"

"Possibly."

Sir Henry's irritation was fast merging into anger.

"I shall turn the fellow out of the house," he declared.

Philippa shrugged her shoulders.

"Why don't you?"

He seated himself on the couch by his wife's side. "Look here, Philippa, don't let's wrangle," he begged. "I'm afraid you'll have to make up your mind to see a good deal less of your friend Lessingham, anyway."

Philippa's brows were knitted. She was conscious of a vague uneasiness.

"Really? And why?"

"For one thing," her husband explained, "because I don't intend to have him hanging about my house during my absence."

"The best way to prevent that would be not to go away," Philippa suggested.

"Well, in all probability," he announced guardedly, "I am not going away again—at least not just yet."

Philippa's manner suddenly changed. She laid down her work. Her hand rested lightly upon her husband's shoulder.

"You mean that you are going to give up those horrible fishing excursions of yours?"

"For the present I am," he assured her.

"And are you going to do something—some work, I mean?" she asked breathlessly.

"For the immediate present I am going to stay at home and look after you," he replied.

Philippa's face fell. Her manner became notably colder.

"You are very wise," she declared. "Mr. Lessingham is a most fascinating person. We are all half in love with him—even Helen."

"The fellow must have a way with him," Sir Henry conceded grudgingly. "As a rule the people here are not over-keen on strangers, unless they have immediate connections in the neighbourhood. Even Griffiths, who since they made him Commandant, is a man of many suspicions, seems inclined to accept him."

"Captain Griffiths dined here the other night," Philippa remarked, "and I noticed that he and Mr. Lessingham seemed to get on very well."

"The fellow's all right in his way, no doubt," Sir Henry began.

"Of course he is," Philippa interrupted. "Helen likes him quite as much as I do."

"Does he make love to Helen, too?" Sir Henry ventured.

"Don't talk nonsense!" Philippa retorted. "He isn't that sort of a man at all. If he has made love to me, he has done so because I have encouraged him, and if I have encouraged him, it is your fault."

Sir Henry, with an impatient exclamation, rose from his place and took a cigarette from an open box.

"Quite time I stayed at home, I can see. All the same, the fellow's rather a puzzle. I can't help wondering how he succeeded in making such an easy conquest of a lady who has scarcely been notorious for her flirtations, and a young woman who is madly in love with another man. He hasn't—"

"Hasn't what?"

"He hasn't," Sir Henry continued, blowing out the match which he had been holding to his cigarette and throwing it away, "been in the position of being able to render you or Helen any service, has he?"

"I don't understand you," Philippa replied, a little uneasily.

"There's nothing to understand," Sir Henry went on. "I was simply trying to find some explanation for his veni, vidi, vici."

"I don't think you need go any further than the fact," Philippa observed, "that he is well-bred, charming and companionable."

"Incidentally," Sir Henry queried, "do you happen to have come across any one here who ever heard of him before?"

"I don't remember any one," Philippa replied. "He was at college with Richard, you know."

Sir Henry nodded.

"Of course, that's a wonderful introduction to you and Helen," he admitted. "And by-the-by, that reminds me," he went on, "I never saw such a change in two women in my life, as in you and Helen. A few weeks ago you were fretting yourselves to death about Dick. Now you don't seem to mention him, you both of you look as though you hadn't a care in the world, and yet you say you haven't heard from him. Upon my word, this is getting to be a house of mysteries!"

"The only mystery in it that I can see, is you, Henry," she declared.

"Me?" he protested. "I'm one of the simplest-minded fellows alive. What is there mysterious about me?"

"Your ignominious life," was the cold reply.

"Jove, I got it that time!" he groaned,—"got it in the neck! But didn't I tell you just now that I was turning over a new leaf?"

"Then prove it," Philippa pleaded. "Let me write to Rayton and beg him to use his influence to get you something to do. I am sure you would be happier, and I can't tell you what a difference it would make to me."

"It's that indoor work I couldn't stick, old thing," he confided. "You know, they're saying all the time it's a young man's war. They'd make me take some one's place at home behind a desk."

"But even if they did," she protested, "even if they put you in a coal cellar, wouldn't you be happier to feel that you were helping your country? Wouldn't you be glad to know that I was happier?"

Sir Henry made a wry face.

"It seems to me that your outlook is a trifle superficial, dear," he grumbled. "However—now what the dickens is the matter?"

The door had been opened by Mills, with his usual smoothness, but Jimmy Dumble, out of breath and excited, pushed his way into the room.

"Hullo? What is it, Jimmy?" his patron demanded.

"Beg your pardon, sir," was the almost incoherent reply. "I've run all the way up, and there's a rare wind blowing. There's one of our—our trawlers lying off the Point, and she's sent up three green and six yellow balls."

"Whiting, by God!" Sir Henry exclaimed.

"Whiting!" Philippa repeated, in agonised disgust. "What does this mean, Henry?"

"It must be a shoal," her husband explained. "It means that we've got to get amongst them quick. Is the Ida down on the beach, Jimmy?"

"She there all right, sir," was the somewhat doubtful reply, "but us'll have a rare job to get away, sir. That there nor'easter is blowing great guns again and it's a cruel tide."

"We've got to get out somehow," Sir Henry declared. "Mills, my oilskins and flask at once. I sha'n't change a thing, but you might bring a cardigan jacket and the whisky and soda."

Mills withdrew, a little dazed. Philippa, whose fingers were clenched together, found her tongue at last.

"Henry!" she exclaimed furiously.

"What is it, my dear?"

"Do you mean to tell me that after your promise," she continued, "after what you have just said, you are starting out to-night for another fishing expedition?"

"Whiting, my dear," Sir Henry explained. "One can't possibly miss whiting. Where the devil are my keys?—Here they are. Now then."

He sat down before his desk, took some papers from the top drawer, rummaged about for a moment or two in another, and found what seemed to be a couple of charts in oilskin cases. All the time the wind was shaking the windows, and a storm of rain was beating against the panes.

"Help yourself to whisky and soda, Jimmy," Sir Henry invited, as he buttoned up his coat. "You'll need it all presently."

"I thank you kindly, sir," Jimmy replied. "I am thinking that we'll both need a drink before we're through this night."

He helped himself to a whisky and soda on the generous principle of half and half. Philippa, who was watching her husband's preparations indignantly, once more found words.

"Henry, you are incorrigible!" she exclaimed. "Listen to me if you please. I insist upon it."

Sir Henry turned a little impatiently towards her. "Philippa, I really can't stop now," he protested. "But you must! You shall!" she cried. "You shall hear this much from me, at any rate, before you go. What I said the other day I repeat a thousandfold now."

Sir Henry glanced at Dumble and motioned his head towards the door. The fisherman made an awkward exit.

"A thousandfold," Philippa repeated passionately. "You hear, Henry? I do not consider myself any more your wife. If I am here when you return, it will be simply because I find it convenient. Your conduct is disgraceful and unmanly."

"My dear girl!" he remonstrated. "I may be back in twenty-four—possibly twelve hours."

"It is a matter of indifference to me when you return," was the curt reply. "I have finished."

The door was thrown open.

"Your oilskins, sir, and flask," Mills announced, hurrying in, a little breathless. "You'll forgive my mentioning it, sir, but it scarcely seems a fit night to leave home."

"Got to be done this once, Mills," his master replied, struggling into his coat.

The young people from the billiard room suddenly streamed in. Nora, who was still carrying her cue, gazed at her father in amazement.

"Why, where's Dad going?" she cried.

"It appears," Philippa explained sarcastically, "that a shoal of whiting has arrived."

"Very uncertain fish, whiting," Sir Henry observed, "here to-day and gone to-morrow."

"You won't find it too easy getting off to-night, sir," Harrison remarked doubtfully.

"Jimmy will see to that," was the confident reply. "I expect we shall be amongst them at daybreak. Good-by, everybody! Good-by, Philippa!"

His eyes sought his wife's in vain. She had turned towards Lessingham.

"You are not hurrying off, are you, Mr. Lessingham?" she asked. "I want you to show me that new Patience."

"I shall be delighted."

Sir Henry turned slowly away. For a moment his face darkened as his eyes met Lessingham's. He seemed about to speak but changed his mind.

"Well, good-by, every one," he called out. "I shall be back before midnight if we don't get out."

"And if you do?" Nora cried.

"If we do, Heaven help the whiting!"

CHAPTER XV

"Of course, we're behaving shockingly, all three of us!" Philippa declared, as she sipped her champagne and leaned back in her seat.

"You mean by coming to a place like this?" Lessingham queried, looking around the crowded restaurant. "We are not, in that case, the only sinners."

"I didn't mean the mere fact of being here," Philippa explained, "but being here with you."

"I forgot," he said gloomily, "that I was such a black sheep."

"Don't be silly," she admonished. "You're nothing of the sort. But, of course, we are skating on rather thin ice. If I had Henry to consider in any way, if he had any sort of a career, perhaps I should be more careful. As it is, I think I feel a little reckless lately. Dreymarsh has got upon my nerves. The things that I thought most of in life seem to have crumbled away."

"Ought I to be sorry?" he asked. "I am not."

"But why are you so unsympathetic?"

"Because I am waiting by your side to rebuild," he whispered.

A tall, bronzed young soldier with his arm in a sling, stopped before their table, and Helen, after a moment's protest and a glance at Philippa, moved away with him to the little space reserved for the dancers.

"What a chaperon I am!" Philippa sighed. "I scarcely know anything about the young man except his name and that he was in Dick's regiment."

"I did not hear it," Lessingham observed, "but I feel deeply grateful to him. It is so seldom that I have a chance to talk to you alone like this."

"It seems incredible that we have talked so long," Philippa said, glancing at the watch upon her wrist. "I really feel now that I know all about you—your school days, your college days, and your soldiering. You have been very frank, haven't you?"

"I have nothing to conceal—from you," he replied. "If there is anything more you want to know—"

"There is nothing," she interrupted uneasily.

"Perhaps you are wise," he reflected, "and yet some day, you know, you will have to hear it all, over and over again."

"I will not be made love to in a restaurant," she declared firmly.

"You are so particular as to localities," he complained. "You could not see your way clear, I suppose, to suggest what you would consider a suitable environment?"

Philippa looked at him for a moment very earnestly.

"Ah, don't let us play at things we neither of us feel!" she begged. "And there is some one there who wants to speak to you."

Lessingham looked up into the face of the man who had paused before their table, as one might look into the face of unexpected death. He remained perfectly still, but the slight colour seemed slowly to be drawn from his cheeks. Yet the newcomer himself seemed in no way terrifying. He was tall and largely built, clean-shaven, and with the humourous mouth of an Irishman or an American. Neither was there anything threatening in his speech.

"Glad to run up against you, Lessingham," he said, holding out his hand. "Gay crowd here tonight, isn't it?"

"Very," Lessingham answered, speaking very much like a man in a dream. "Lady Cranston, will you permit me to introduce my friend—Mr. Hayter."

Philippa was immediately gracious, and a few moments passed in trivial conversation. Then Mr. Hayter prepared to depart.

"I must be joining my friends," he observed. "Look in and see me sometime, Lessingham—Number 72, Milan Court. You know what a nightbird I am. Perhaps you will call and have a final drink with me when you have finished here."

"I shall be very glad," Lessingham promised.

Mr. Hayter passed on, a man, apparently, of many acquaintances, to judge by his interrupted progress. Lady Cranston looked at her companion. She was puzzled.

"Is that a recent acquaintance," she asked, "as he addressed you by the name of Lessingham?"

"Yes," was the quiet reply.

"You don't wish to talk about him?"

"No!"

Helen and her partner returned, a few moments later, and the little party presently broke up. Lessingham drove the two women to their hotel in Dover Street.

"We've had a most delightful evening," Philippa assured him, as they said good night. "You are coming round to see us in the morning, aren't you?"

"If I may," Lessingham assented.

Helen found her way into Philippa's room, later on that night. She had nerved herself for a very thankless task.

"May I sit down for a few moments?" she asked, a little nervously. "Your fire is so much better than mine."

Philippa glanced at her friend through the looking-glass before which she was brushing her hair, and made a little grimace. She felt a forewarning of what was coming.

"Of course, dear," she replied. "Have you enjoyed your evening?"

"Very much, in a way," was the somewhat hesitating reply. "Of course, nothing really counts until Dick comes back, but it is nice to talk with some one who knows him."

"Agreeable conversation," Philippa remarked didactically, "is one of the greatest pleasures in life."

"You find Mr. Lessingham very interesting, don't you?" Helen asked.

Philippa finished arranging her hair to her satisfaction and drew up an easy-chair opposite her visitor's.

"So you want to talk with me about Mr. Lessingham, do you?"

"I suppose you know that he's in love with you?" Helen began.

"I hope he is a little, my dear," was the smiling reply. "I'm sure I've tried my best."

"Won't you talk seriously?" Helen pleaded.

"I don't altogether see the necessity," Philippa protested.

"I do, and I'll tell you why," Helen answered. "I don't think Mr. Lessingham is at all the type of man to which you are accustomed. I think that he is in deadly earnest about you. I think that he was in deadly earnest from the first. You don't really care for him, do you, dear?"

"Very much, and yet not, perhaps, quite in the way you are thinking of," was the quiet reply.

"Then please send him away," Helen begged.

"My dear, how can I?" Philippa objected. "He has done us an immense service, and he can't disobey his orders."

"You don't want him to go away, then?"

Philippa was silent for several moments. "No," she admitted, "I don't think that I do."

"You don't care for Henry any more?"

"Just as much as ever," was the somewhat bitter reply. "That's what I resent so much. I should like Henry to believe that he had killed every spark of love in me."

Helen moved across and sat on the arm of her friend's chair. She felt that she was going to be very daring.

"Have you any idea at the back of your mind, dear," she asked "of making use of Mr. Lessingham to punish Henry?"

Philippa moved a little uneasily.

"How hatefully downright you are!" she murmured. "I don't know."

"Because," Helen continued, "if you have any such idea in your mind, I think it is most unfair to Mr. Lessingham. You know perfectly well that anything else between you and him would be impossible."

"And why?"

"Don't be ridiculous!" Helen exclaimed vigorously. "Mr. Lessingham may have all the most delightful qualities in the world, but he has attached himself to a country which no English man or woman will be able to think of without shuddering, for many years to come. You can't dream of cutting yourself adrift from your friends and your home and your country! It's too unnatural! I'm not even arguing with you, Philippa. You couldn't do it! I'm wholly concerned with Mr. Lessingham. I cannot forget what we owe him. I think it would be hatefully cruel of you to spoil his life."

Philippa's flashes of seriousness were only momentary. She made a little grimace. She was once more her natural, irresponsible self.

"You underrate my charm, Helen," she declared. "I really believe that I could make his life instead of spoiling it."

"And you would pay the price?"

Philippa, slim and elflike in the firelight, rose from her chair. There was a momentary cruelty in her face.

"I sometimes think," she said calmly, "that I would pay any price in the world to make Henry understand how I feel. There, now run along, dear. You're full of good intentions, and don't think it horrid of me, but nothing that you could say would make any difference."

"You wouldn't do anything rash?" Helen pleaded.

"Well, if I run away with Mr. Lessingham, I certainly can't promise that I'll send cards out first. Whatever I do, impulse will probably decide."

"Impulse!"

"Why not? I trust mine. Can't you?" Philippa added, with a little shrug of the shoulders.

"Sometimes," Helen sighed, "they are such wild horses, you know. They lead one to such terrible places."

"And sometimes," Philippa replied, "they find their way into the heaven where our soberer thoughts could never take us. Good night, dear!"

CHAPTER XVI

Mr. William Hayter, in the solitude of his chambers at the Milan Court, was a very altered personage. He extended no welcoming salutation to his midnight visitor but simply motioned him to a chair.

"Well," he began, "is your task finished that you are in London?"

"My task," Lessingham replied, "might just as well never have been entered upon. The man you sent me to watch is nothing but an ordinary sport-loving Englishman."

"Really! You have lived as his neighbour for nearly a month, and that is your impression of him?"

"It is," Lessingham assented. "He has been away sea-fishing, half the time, but I have searched his house thoroughly."

"Searched his papers, eh?"

"Every one I could find, and hated the job. There are a good many charts of the coast, but they are all for the use of the fishermen."

"Wonderful!" Hayter scoffed. "My young friend, you may yet find distinction in some other walk of life. Our secret service, I fancy, will very soon be able to dispense with your energies."

"And I with your secret service," Lessingham agreed heartily. "I dare say there may be some branches of it in which existence is tolerable. That, however, does not apply to the task upon which I have been engaged."

"You have been completely duped," Hayter told him calmly, "and the information you have sent us is valueless. Sir Henry Cranston, instead of being the type of man whom you have described, is one of the greatest experts upon coast defense and mine-laying, in the English Admiralty."

Lessingham laughed shortly.

"That," he declared, "is perfectly absurd."

"It is," Hayter repeated, with emphasis, "the precise truth. Sir Henry Cranton's fishing excursions are myths. He is simply transferred from his fishing boat on to one of a little fleet of so-called mine sweepers, from which he conducts his operations. Nearly every one of the most important towns on the east coast are protected by minefields of his design."

Lessingham was dumbfounded. His companion's manner was singularly convincing.

"But how could Sir Henry or any one else keep this a secret?" he protested. "Even his wife is scarcely on speaking terms with him because she believes him to be an idler, and the whole neighbourhood gossips over his slackness."

"The whole neighbourhood is easily fooled," Hayter retorted. "There are one or two who know, however."

"There are one or two," Lessingham observed grimly, "who are beginning to suspect me."

"That is a pity," Hayter admitted, "because it will be necessary for you to return to Dreymarsh at once."

"Return to Dreymarsh at once? But Cranston is away. There is nothing for me to do there in his absence."

"He will be back on Wednesday or Thursday night," was the confident reply. "He will bring with him the plan of his latest defenses of a town on the east coast, which our cruiser squadron purpose to bombard. We must have that chart."

Lessingham listened in mute distress.

"Could you possibly get me relieved?" he begged. "The fact is—"

"We could not, and we will not," Hayter interrupted fiercely. "Unless you wish me to denounce you at home as a renegade and a coward, you will go through with the work which has been allotted to you. Your earlier mistakes will be forgiven if that chart is in my hands by Friday."

"But how do you know that he will have it?" Lessingham protested. "Supposing you are right and he is really responsible for the minefields you speak of, I should think the last thing he would do would be to bring the chart back to Dreymarsh."

"As a matter of fact, that is precisely what he will do," Hayter assured his listener. "He is bringing it back for the inspection of one of the commissioners for the east coast defense, who is to meet him at his house. And I wish to warn you, too, Maderstrom, that you will have very little time. For some reason or other, Cranston is dissatisfied with the secrecy under which he has been compelled to work, and has applied to the Admiralty for recognition of his position. Immediately this is given, I gather that his house will be inaccessible to you."

Lessingham sat, his arms folded, his eyes fixed upon the fire. His thoughts were in a turmoil, yet one thing was hatefully clear. Cranston was not the unworthy slacker he had believed him to be. Philippa's whole point of view might well be changed by this discovery—especially now that Cranston had made up his mind to assert himself for his wife's sake. There was an icy fear in his heart.

"You understand," Hayter persisted coldly, "what it is you have to do?"

"Perfectly. I shall return by the afternoon train," was the despairing reply.

"If you succeed," Hayter continued, "I shall see that you get the usual acknowledgment, but I will, if you wish it, ask for your transfer to another branch of the service. I am not questioning your patriotism or your honour, Maderstrom, but you are not the man for this work."

"You are right," Lessingham said. "I am not."

"It is not my affair," Hayter proceeded, "to enquire too closely into the means used by our agents in carrying out our designs. That I find you in London in company with the wife of the man whom you are appointed to watch, may be a fact capable of the most complete and satisfactory explanation. I ask no questions. I only remind you that your country, even though it be only your adopted country, demands from you, as from all others in her service, unswerving loyalty, a loyalty uninfluenced by the claims of personal sentiment, duty, or honour. Have I said enough?"

"You have said as much as it is wise for you to say," Lessingham replied, his voice trembling with suppressed passion.

"That is all, then," the other concluded. "You know where to send or bring the chart when you have it? If you bring it yourself, it is possible that something which you may regard as a reward, will be offered to you."

Lessingham rose a little wearily to his feet. His farewell to Hayter was cold and lifeless.

He left the hotel and started on his homeward way, struggling with a sense of intolerable depression. The streets through which he passed were sombre and unlit.

A Zeppelin warning, a few hours before, had driven the people to their homes. There was not a chink of light to be seen anywhere. An intense and gloomy stillness seemed to brood over the deserted thoroughfares. Nightbirds on their way home flitted by like shadows. Policemen lurked in the shadows of the houses. The few vehicles left crawled about with insufficient lights. Even the warning horns of the taxicab men sounded furtive and repressed. Lessingham, as he marched stolidly along, felt curiously in sympathy with his environment. Hayter's news brought him face to face with that inner problem which had so suddenly become the dominant factor in his life. For the first time he knew what love was. He felt the wonder of it, the far-reaching possibilities, the strange idealism called so unexpectedly into being. He recognized the vagaries of Philippa's disposition, and yet, during the last few days, he had convinced himself that she was beginning to care. Her strained relations with her husband had been, without a doubt, her first incentive towards the acceptance of his proffered devotion. Now he told himself with eager hopefulness that some portion of it, however minute, must be for his own sake. The relations between husband and wife, he reminded himself, must, at any rate, have been strained during the last few months, or Cranston would never have been able to keep his secret. In his gloomy passage through this land of ill omens, however, he shivered a little as he thought of the other possibility—tortured himself with imagining what might happen during her revulsion of feeling, if Philippa discovered the truth. A sense of something greater than he had yet known in life seemed to lift him into some lofty state of aloofness, from which he could look down and despise himself, the poor, tired plodder wearing the heavy chains of duty. There was a life so much more wonderful, just the other side of the clouds, a very short distance away, a life of alluring and passionate happiness. Should he ever find the courage, he wondered, to escape from the treadmill and go in search of it? Duty, for the last two years, had taken him by the hand and led him along a pathway of shame. He had never been a hypocrite about the war. He was one of those who had acknowledged from the first that Germany had set forth, with the sword in her hand, on a war of conquest. His own inherited martial spirit had vaguely approved; he, too, in those earlier days, had felt the sunlight upon his rapier. Later had come the enlightenment, the turbulent waves of doubt, the nightmare of a nation's awakening conscience, mirrored in his own soul. It was in a depression shared, perhaps, in a lesser degree by millions of those whose ranks he had joined, that he felt this passionate craving for escape into a world which took count of other things.

CHAPTER XVII

Punctually at 12 o'clock the next morning, Lessingham presented himself at the hotel in Dover Street and was invited by the hall porter to take a seat in the lounge. Philippa entered, a few minutes later, her eyes and cheeks brilliant with the brisk exercise she had been taking, her slim figure most becomingly arrayed in grey cloth and chinchilla.

"I lost Helen in Harrod's," she announced, "but I know she's lunching with friends, so it really doesn't matter. You'll have to take care of me, Mr. Lessingham, until the train goes, if you will."

"For even longer than that, if you will," he murmured.

She laughed. "More pretty speeches? I don't think I'm equal to them before luncheon."

"This time I am literal," he explained. "I am coming back to Dreymarsh myself."

He felt his heart beat quicker, a sudden joy possessed him. Philippa's expression was obviously one of satisfaction.

"I'm so glad," she assured him. "Do you know, I was thinking only as I came back in the taxicab, how I should miss you."

She was standing with her foot upon the broad fender, and her first little impulse of pleasure seemed to pass as she looked into the fire. She turned towards him gravely.

"After all, do you think you are wise?" she asked. "Of course, I don't think that any one at Dreymarsh has the least suspicion, but you know Captain Griffiths did ask questions, and—well, you're safely away now. You have been so wonderful about Dick, so wonderful altogether," she went on, "that I couldn't bear it if trouble were to come."

He smiled at her.

"I think I know what is at the back of your mind," he said. "You think that I am coming back entirely on your account. As it happens, this is not so."

She looked at him with wide-open eyes.

"Surely," she exclaimed, "you have satisfied yourself that there is no field for your ingenuity in Dreymarsh?"

"I thought that I had," he admitted. "It seems that I am wrong. I have had orders to return."

"Orders to return?" she repeated. "From whom?"

He shook his head.

"Of course, I ought not to have asked that," she proceeded hastily, "but it does seem odd to realise that you can receive instructions and messages from Germany, here in London."

"Very much the same sort of thing goes on in Germany," he reminded her.

"So they say," she admitted, "but one doesn't come into contact with it. So you are really coming back to Dreymarsh!"

"With you, if I may?"

"Naturally," she agreed.

He glanced at the clock. "We might almost be starting for lunch," he suggested.

She nodded. "As soon as I've told Grover about the luggage."

She was absent only a few moments, and then, as it was a dry, sunny morning, they walked down St. James Street and along Pall Mall to the Carlton. Philippa met several acquaintances, but Lessingham walked with his head erect, looking neither to the right nor to the left.

"Aren't you sometimes afraid of being recognised?" she asked him. "There must be a great many men about of your time at Magdalen, for instance?"

"Nine years makes a lot of difference," he reminded her, "and besides, I have a theory that it is only when the eyes meet that recognition really takes place. So long as I do not look into any one's face, I feel quite safe."

"You are sure that you would not like to go to a smaller place than the Carlton?"

"It makes no difference," he assured her. "My credentials have been wonderfully established for me."

"I'm so glad," she confessed. "I know it's most unfashionable, but I do like these big places. If ever I had my way, I should like to live in London and have a cottage in the country, instead of living in the country and being just an hotel dweller in London."

"I wonder if New York would not do?" he ventured.

"I expect I should like New York," she murmured.

"I think," he said, "in fact, I am almost sure that when I leave here I shall go to the United States."

She looked at him and turned suddenly away. They arrived just then at their destination, and the moment passed. Lessingham left his companion in the lounge while he went back into the restaurant to secure his table and order lunch. When he came back, he found Philippa sitting very upright and with a significant glitter in her eyes.

"Look over there," she whispered, "by the palm."

He followed the direction which she indicated. A man was standing against one of the pillars, talking to a tall, dark woman, obviously a foreigner, wrapped in wonderful furs. There was something familiar about his figure and the slight droop of his head.

"Why, it's Sir Henry!" Lessingham exclaimed, as the man turned around.

"My husband," Philippa faltered.

Sir Henry, if indeed it were he, seemed afflicted with a sudden shortsightedness. He met the incredulous gaze both of Lessingham and his wife without recognition or any sign of flinching. At that distance it was impossible to see the tightening of his lips and the steely flash in his blue eyes.

"The whiting seem to have brought him a long way," Philippa said, with an unnatural little laugh.

"Shall I go and speak to him?" Lessingham asked.

"For heaven's sake, no!" she insisted. "Don't leave me. I wouldn't have him come near me for anything in the world. It is only a few weeks ago that I begged him to come to London with me, and he said that he hated the place. You don't know—the woman?"

Lessingham shook his head.

"She looks like a foreigner," was all he could say.

"Take me in to lunch at once," Philippa begged, rising abruptly to her feet. "This is really the last straw."

They passed up the stairway and within a few feet of where Sir Henry was standing. He appeared absorbed, however, in conversation with his companion, and did not even turn around. Philippa's little face seemed to have hardened as she took her seat. Only her eyes were still unnaturally bright.

"I am so sorry if this has annoyed you," Lessingham regretted. "You would not care to go elsewhere?"

"I? Go anywhere else?" she exclaimed scornfully. "Thank you, I am perfectly satisfied here. And with my companion," she added, with a brilliant little smile. "Now tell me about New York. Have you ever been there?"

"Twice," he told her. "At present the dream of my life is to go there with you."

She looked at him a little wonderingly.

"I wonder if you really care," she said. "Men get so much into the habit of saying that sort of thing to women. Sometimes it seems to me they must do a great deal of mischief. But you—Is that really your wish?"

"I would sacrifice everything that I have ever held dear in life," he declared, with his face aglow, "for its realization."

"But you would be a deserter from your country," she pointed out. "You would never be able to return. Your estates would be confiscated. You would be homeless."

"Home," he said softly, "is where one's heart takes one. Home is just where love is."

Her eyes, as they met his, were for a moment suspiciously soft. Then she began to talk very quickly of other things, to compare notes of countries which they had both visited, even of people whom they had met. They were obliged to leave early to catch their train. As they passed down the crowded restaurant they once more found themselves within a few feet of Sir Henry. His back was turned to them, and he was apparently ignorant of their near presence. The party had become a partie Carrée, another man, and a still younger and more beautiful woman having joined it.

"Of course," Philippa said, as they descended the stairs, "I am behaving like an idiot. I ought to go and tell Henry exactly what I think of him, or pull him away in the approved Whitechapel fashion. We lose so much, don't we, by stifling our instincts."

"For the next few minutes," he replied, glancing at his watch, "I think we had better concentrate our attention upon catching our train."

They reached King's Cross with only a few minutes to spare. Grover, however, had already secured a carriage, and Helen was waiting for them, ensconced in a corner. She accepted the news of Lessingham's return with resignation. Philippa became thoughtful as they drew towards the close of their journey and the slow, frosty twilight began to creep down upon the land.

"I suppose we don't really know what war is," she observed, looking out of the window at a comfortable little village tucked away with a background of trees and guarded by a weather-beaten old church. "The people are safe in their homes. You must appreciate what that means, Mr. Lessingham."

"Indeed I do," he answered gravely. "I have seen the earth torn and dismembered as though by the plough of some destroying angel. A few blackened ruins where, an hour or so before, a peaceful village stood; men and women running about like lunatics stricken with a mortal fear. And all the time a red glow on the horizon, a blood-red glow, and little specks of grey or brown lying all over the fields; even the cattle racing round in terror. And every now and then the cry of Death! You are fortunate in England."

Philippa leaned forward.

"Do you believe that our turn will come?" she asked. "Do you believe that the wave will break over our country?"

"Who can tell?"

"Ah, no, but answer me," she begged. "Is it possible for you to land an army here?"

"I think," he replied, "that all things are possible to the military genius of Germany. The only question is whether it is worth while. Germans are supposed to be sentimentalists, you know. I rather doubt it. There is nothing would set the joybells of Berlin clanging so much as the news of a German invasion of Great Britain. On the other hand, there is a great party in Germany, and a very far-seeing one, which is continually reminding the Government that, without Great Britain as a market, Germany would never recover from the financial strain of the war."

"This is all too impersonal," Philippa objected. "Do you, in your heart, believe that the time might come when in the night we should hear the guns booming in Dreymarsh Bay, and see your grey-clad soldiers forming up on the beach and scaling our cliffs?"

"That will not be yet," he pronounced. "It has been thought of. Once it was almost attempted. Just at present, no."

Philippa drew a sigh of relief.

"Then your mission in Dreymarsh has nothing to do with an attempted landing?"

"Nothing," he assured her. "I can even go a little further. I can tell you that if ever we do try to land, it will be in an unsuspected place, in an unexpected fashion."

"Well, it's really very comforting to hear these things at first-hand," Philippa declared, with some return to her usual manner. "I suppose we are really two disgraceful women, Helen and I—traitors and all the rest of it. Here we sit talking to an enemy as though he were one of our best friends."

"I refuse to be called an enemy," Lessingham protested. "There are times when individuality is a far greater thing than nationality. I am just a human being, born into the same world and warmed by the same sun as you. Nothing can alter the fact that we are fellow creatures."

"Dreymarsh once more," Philippa announced, looking out of the window. "And you're a terribly plausible person, Mr. Lessingham. Come round and see us after dinner—if it doesn't interfere with your work."

"On the contrary," he murmured under his breath. "Thank you very much."

CHAPTER XVIII

Sir Henry was standing with his hands in his pockets and a very blank expression upon his face, looking out upon the Admiralty Square. He was alone in a large, barely furnished apartment, the walls of which were so hung with charts that it had almost the appearance of a schoolroom prepared for an advanced geography class. The table from which he had risen was covered with an amazing number of scientific appliances, some samples of rock and sand, two microscopes and several telephones.

Sir Henry, having apparently exhausted the possibilities of the outlook, turned somewhat reluctantly away to find himself confronted by an elderly gentleman of cheerful appearance, who at that moment had entered the room. From the fact that he had done so without knocking, it was obvious that he was an intimate.

"Well, my gloomy friend," the newcomer demanded, "what's wrong with you?"

Sir Henry was apparently relieved to see his visitor. He pushed a chair towards him and indicated with a gesture of invitation a box of cigars upon his desk.

"Your little Laranagas," he observed. "Try one."

The visitor opened the box, sniffed at its contents, and helped himself.

"Now, then, get at it, Henry," he enjoined. "I've a Board in half-an-hour, and three dispatches to read before I go in. What's your trouble?"

"Look here, Rayton," was the firm reply, "I want to chuck this infernal hole-and-corner business. I tell you I've worked it threadbare at Dreymarsh and it's getting jolly uncomfortable."

The newcomer grinned.

"Poor chap!" he observed, watching his cigar smoke curl upwards. "You're in a nasty mess, you know, Henry. Did I tell you that I had a letter from your wife the other day, asking me if I couldn't find you a job?"

Sir Henry waited a little grimly, whilst his friend enjoyed the joke.

"That's all very well," he said, "but we are on the point of a separation, or something of the sort. I'll admit it was all right at first to run the thing on the Q.T., but that's pretty well busted up by now. Why, according to your own reports, they know all about me on the other side."

"Not a doubt about it," the other agreed. "I'm not sure that you haven't got a spy fellow down at Dreymarsh now."

"I'm quite sure of it," Sir Henry replied grimly. "The brute was lunching with my wife at the Carlton to-day, and, as luck would have it, I was landed with that Russian Admiral's wife and sister-in-law. You're breaking up the happy home, that's what you're doing, Rayton!"

His lordship at any rate seemed to find the process amusing. He laughed until the tears stood in his eyes.

"I should love to have seen Philippa's face," he chuckled, "when she walked into the restaurant and saw you there! You're supposed to be off on a fishing expedition, aren't you?"

"I went out after whiting," Sir Henry groaned, "and I'd just promised to chuck it for a time when I got the Admiral's message."

"Well, we'll see to your German spy, anyway," his visitor promised.

"Don't be an ass!" Sir Henry exclaimed irritably. "I don't want the fellow touched at present. Why, he's been a sort of persona grata at my house. Hangs around there all the time when I'm away."

"All the more reason for putting an end to his little game, I should say," was the cheerful reply.

"And have the whole neighbourhood either laughing at my wife and Miss Fairclough, or talking scandal about them!" Sir Henry retorted.

"I forgot that," his friend confessed ruminatively. "He's a gentlemanly sort of fellow, from what I hear, but a rotten spy. What do you want done with him?"

"Leave him for me to deal with," Sir Henry insisted. "I have a little scheme on hand in which he is concerned."

Rayton scratched his chin doubtfully.

"The fellow may not be such a fool as he seems," he reminded his friend.

"I won't run any risks," Sir Henry promised. "I just want him left there, that's all. And look here, Rayton, you know what I want from you. I quite agreed to your proposals as to my anonymity at the time when I was up in Scotland, but the thing's a secret no longer with the people who count. Every one in Germany knows that I'm a mine-field specialist, so I don't see why the dickens I should pose any longer as a sort of half-baked idiot."

Rayton's eyes twinkled.

"You want to play the Wilson Barrett hero and make a theatrical disclosure of your greatness," he laughed. "Poor Philippa will fall upon her knees. You will be the hero of the village, which will probably present you with some little article of plate. You've a good time coming, Henry."

"Talk sense, there's a good fellow," the other begged. "You go and see the Chief and put it to him. There isn't a single reason why I shouldn't own up now."

"I'll see what I can do," Rayton promised, "but what about this fellow Lessingham, or whatever else he calls himself, down there? There's a chap named Griffiths—Commandant, isn't he?—been writing us about him."

"I won't have Lessingham touched," Sir Henry insisted. "He can't do any particular harm down there, and there isn't a line or a drawing of mine down at Dreymarsh which he isn't welcome to."

Lord Rayton rose to his feet.

"Look here, Henry, old fellow," he said, "I do sympathise with you up to a certain point. I tell you what I'll do. I shall have to answer Philippa's letter, and I'll answer it in such a way that if she is as clever a little woman as I think she is, she'll get a hint. Of course," he went on ruminatively, "it is rather a misfortune that the Princess Ollaneff and her sister are such jolly good-looking women. Makes it look a little fishy, doesn't it? What I mean to say is, it's a far cry from fishing for whiting in the North Sea to lunching with a beautiful princess at the Carlton—when you think your wife's down in Norfolk."

Sir Henry threw open the door.

"Look here, I've had enough of you, Rayton," he declared. "You get back and do an hour's work, if you can bring your mind to it."

The latter assumed a sudden dignity, necessitated by the sound of voices in the corridor, and departed. The door had scarcely been closed when two younger men presented themselves—Miles Ensol, Sir Henry's secretary, a typical-looking young sailor minus his left arm; and a pale-faced, clean-shaven man of uncertain age, in civilian clothes. Sir Henry shook hands with the latter and pointed to the easy-chair which his previous visitor had just vacated.

"Welcome back again, Horridge," he said cordially. "Miles, I'll ring when I want you."

"Very good, sir," the secretary replied. "There's a fisherman from Norfolk downstairs, when you're at liberty."

Sir Henry nodded.

"I'll see him presently. Shut him up somewhere where he can smoke."

The young man withdrew, carefully closing the door, around which Sir Henry, with a word of apology, arranged a screen.

"I don't think," he explained, "that eavesdropping extends to these premises, or that our voices could reach outside. Still, a ha'porth of prevention, eh? Have a cigar, Horridge."

"I'm not smoking for a day or two, thank you, sir."

"You look as though they'd put you through it," Sir Henry remarked.

His visitor smiled.

"I've travelled fourteen miles in a barrel," he said, "and we were out for twenty-four hours in a Danish sailing skiff. You know what the weather's been like in the North Sea. Before that, the last word of writing I saw on German soil was a placard, offering a reward of five thousand marks for my detention, with a disgustingly lifelike photograph at the top. I had about fifty yards of quay to walk in broad daylight, and every other man I passed turned to stare after me. It gives you the cold shivers down your back when you daren't look round to see if you're being followed."

Sir Henry groped in the cupboard of his desk, and produced a bottle of whisky and a syphon of soda water. His visitor nodded approvingly.

"I've touched nothing until I've reached what I consider sanctuary," he observed. "My nerves have gone rotten for the first time in my life. Do you mind, sir, if I lock the door?"

"Go ahead," Sir Henry assented.

He brought the whisky and soda himself across the room. Horridge resumed his seat and held out his hand almost eagerly. For a moment or two he shook as though he had an ague. Then, just as suddenly as it had come upon him, the fit passed. He drained the contents of the tumbler at a gulp, set it down empty by his side, and stretched out his hand for a cigar.

"The end of my journey didn't help matters any," he went on. "I daren't even make for a Dutch port, and we were picked up eventually by a tramp steamer from Newcastle to London with coals. I hadn't been on board more than an hour before a submarine which had been following overhauled us. I thought it was all up then, but the fog lifted, and we found ourselves almost in the midst of a squadron of destroyers from Harwich. I made another transfer, and they landed me in time to catch the early morning train from Felixstowe."

"Did they get the submarine?" his listener asked eagerly.

"Get it!" the other repeated, with a smile. "They blew it into scrap metal."

"Plenty of movement in your life!"

"I've run the gauntlet over there once too often," Horridge said grimly. "Just look at me now, Sir Henry. I'm twenty-nine years old, and it's only two years and a half since I was invalided out of the navy and took this job on. The last person I asked to guess my age put me down at fifty. What should you have said?"

"Somewhere near it," was the candid admission. "Never mind, Horridge, you've done your bit. You shall pass on your experience to a new hand, take your pension and try the south coast of England for a few months. Now let's get on with it. You know what I want to hear about."

Horridge produced from his pocket a long strip of paper.

"They're there, sir," he announced, "coaled to the scuppers, every man standing to stations and steam up. There's the list."

He handed the paper across to Sir Henry, who glanced it down.

"The fast cruiser squadron," he observed. "Hm! Three new ships we haven't any note of. No transports, then, Horridge?'"

"Not a sign of one, sir," was the reply. "They're after a bombardment."

He rose to his feet, walked to a giant map of England, and touched a certain port on the east coast. Sir Henry's eyes glistened.

"You're sure?"

"It is a certainty," Horridge replied. "I've been on three of those ships. I've dined with four of the officers. They're under sealed orders, and the crew believes that they're going to escort out half a dozen commerce destroyers. But I have the truth. That's their objective," Horridge repeated, touching once more the spot upon the map, "and they are waiting just for one thing."

Sir Henry smiled thoughtfully.

"I know what they're waiting for," he said. "Perhaps if they'd a Herr Horridge to send over here for it, they'd have got it before now. As it is—well, I'm not sure," he went on. "It seems a pity to disappoint them, doesn't it? I'd love to give them a run for their money."

Horridge smiled faintly. He knew a good deal about his companion.

"They're spoiling for it, sir," he admitted. Sir Henry spoke down a telephone and a few minutes later Ensol reappeared.

"Find Mr. Horridge a comfortable room," his chief directed, "and one of our confidential typists. You can make out your report at your leisure," he went on. "Come in and see me when it's all finished."

"Certainly, sir," Horridge replied, rising.

Sir Henry held out his hand. He looked with something like wonder at the nerve-shattered man who had risen to his feet with a certain air of briskness.

"Horridge," he said, "I wish I had your pluck."

"I don't know any one in the service from whom you need borrow any, sir," was the quiet reply.

CHAPTER XIX

Lessingham sat upon a fallen tree on Dutchman's Common near the scene of his romantic descent, and looked rather ruefully over the moorland, seawards. Above him, the sky was covered with little masses of quickly scudding clouds. A fugitive and watery sunshine shone feebly upon a wind-tossed sea and a rain-sodden landscape. He found a certain grim satisfaction in comparing the disorderliness of the day with the tumult in his own life. He felt that he had embarked upon an enterprise greater than his capacity, for which he was in many ways entirely unsuitable. And behind him was the scourge of the telegram which he had received a few hours ago, a telegram harmless enough to all appearance, but which, decoded, was like a scourge to his back.

Your work is unsatisfactory and your slackness deserves reprobation. Great events wait upon you. The object of your search is necessary for our imminent operations.

The sound of a horse's hoofs disturbed him. Captain Griffiths, on a great bay mare, glanced curiously at the lonely figure by the roadside, and then pulled up.

"Back again, Mr. Lessingham?" he remarked.

"As you see."

The Commandant fidgeted with his horse for a moment. Then he approached a little nearer to Lessingham's side.

"You are a good walker, I perceive, Mr. Lessingham," he remarked.

"When the fancy takes me," was the equable reply.

"Have you come out to see our new guns?"

"I had no idea," Lessingham answered indifferently, "that you had any."

Griffiths smiled.

"We have a small battery of anti-aircraft guns, newly arrived from the south of England," he said. "The secret of their coming and their locality has kept the neighbourhood in a state of ferment for the last week."

Lessingham remained profoundly uninterested.

"They most of them spotted the guns," his companion continued, "but not many of them have found the searchlights yet."

"It seems a little late in the year," Lessingham observed, "to be making preparations against Zeppelins."

"Well, they cross here pretty often, you know," Griffiths reminded him. "It's only a matter of a few weeks ago that one almost came to grief on this common. We picked up their observation car not fifty yards from where you are sitting."

"I remember hearing about it," Lessingham acknowledged.

"By-the-by," the Commandant continued, smoothing his horse's neck, "didn't you arrive that evening or the evening after?"

"I believe I did."

"Liverpool Street or King's Cross? The King's Cross train was very nearly held up."

"I didn't come by train at all," Lessingham replied, glancing for a moment into the clouds, "And now I come to think of it, it must have been the evening after."

"Fine county for motoring," Griffiths continued, stroking his horse's head.

"The roads I have been on seem very good," was the somewhat bored admission.

"You haven't a car of your own here, have you?"

"Not at present."

Captain Griffiths glanced between his horse's ears for a few moments. Then he turned once more towards his companion.

"Mr. Lessingham," he said, "you are aware that I am Commandant here?"

"I believe," Lessingham replied, "that Lady Cranston told me so."

"It is my duty, therefore," Griffiths went on, "to take a little more than ordinary interest in casual visitors, especially at this time of the year. The fact that you are well-known to Lady Cranston is, of course, an entirely satisfactory explanation of your presence here. At the same time, there is certain information concerning strangers of which we keep a record, and in your case there is a line or two which we have not been able to fill up."

"If I can be of any service," Lessingham murmured.

"Precisely," the other interrupted. "I knew you would feel like that. Now your arrival here—we have the date, I think—October 6th. As you have just remarked, you didn't come by train. How did you come?"

Lessingham's surprise was apparently quite genuine.

"Is that a question which you ask me to answer—officially?" he enquired.

His interlocutor shrugged his shoulders.

"I am not putting official questions to you at all," he replied, "nor am I cross-examining you, as might be my duty, under the circumstances, simply because your friendship with the Cranstons is, of course, a guarantee as to your position. But on the other hand, I think it would be reasonable if you were to answer my question."

Lessingham nodded.

"Perhaps you are right," he admitted. "As you can tell by finding me here this afternoon, I am a great walker. I arrived—on foot."

"I see," Griffiths reflected. "The other question which we usually ask is, where was your last stopping place?"

"Stopping place?" Lessingham murmured.

"Yes, where did you sleep the night before you came here?" Griffiths persisted.

Lessingham shook his head as though oppressed by some distasteful memory.

"But I did not sleep at all," he complained. "It was one of the worst nights which I have ever spent in my life."

Captain Griffiths gathered up his reins.

"Well," he said with clumsy sarcasm, "I am much obliged to you, Mr. Lessingham, for the straight-forward way in which you have answered my questions. I won't bother you any more just at present. Shall I see you to-morrow night at Mainsail Haul?"

"Lady Cranston has asked me to dine," was the somewhat reserved reply.

His inquisitor nodded and cantered away. Lessingham looked after him until he had disappeared, then he turned his face towards Dreymarsh and walked steadily into the lowering afternoon. Twilight was falling as he reached Mainsail Haul, where he found Philippa entertaining some callers, to whom she promptly introduced him. Lessingham gathered, almost in the first few minutes, that his presence in Dreymarsh was becoming a subject of comment.

"My husband has played bridge with you at the club, I think," a lady by whose side he found himself observed. "You perhaps didn't hear my name—Mrs. Johnson?"

"I congratulate you upon your husband," Lessingham replied. "I remember him perfectly well because he kept his temper when I revoked."

"Dear me!" she exclaimed. "He must have taken a fancy to you, then. As a rule, they rather complain about him at bridge."

"I formed the impression," Lessingham continued, "that he was rather a better player than the majority of the performers there."

Mrs. Johnson, who was a dark and somewhat forbidding-looking lady, smiled.

"He thinks so, at any rate," she conceded. "Didn't he tell me that you were invalided home from the front?"

Lessingham shook his head.

"I am quite sure that it was not mentioned," he said. "We walked home together as far as the hotel one evening, but we spoke only of the golf and some shooting in the neighbourhood."

Philippa, who had been maneuvering to attract Lessingham's attention, suddenly dropped the cake basket which she was passing. There was a little commotion. Lessingham went down on his hands and knees to help collect the fragments, and she found an opportunity to whisper in his ear.

"Be careful. That woman is a cat. Stay and talk to me. Please don't bother, Mr. Lessingham. Won't you ring the bell instead?" she continued, raising her voice.

Lessingham did as he was asked, and affected not to notice Mrs. Johnson's inviting smile as he returned. Philippa made room for him by her side.

"Helen and I were talking this afternoon, Mr. Lessingham," she said, "of the days when you and Dick were both in the Magdalen Eleven and both had just a chance of being chosen for the Varsity. You never played, did you?"

He shook his head.

"No such luck. In any case, Richard would have been in well before me. I always maintained that he was the first of our googlie bowlers."

"So you were at Magdalen with Major Felstead?" another caller remarked in mild wonder.

"Mr. Lessingham and my brother were great friends," Philippa explained. "Mr. Lessingham used to come down to shoot in Cheshire."

Lady Cranston's guests were all conscious of a little indefinable disappointment. The gossip concerning this stranger's appearance in Dreymarsh was practically strangled. Mrs. Johnson, however, fired a parting shot as she rose to go.

"You were not in the same regiment as Major Felstead, were you, Mr. Lessingham?" she asked. "No," he answered calmly.

Philippa was busy with her adieux. Mrs. Johnson remained indomitable.

"What was your regiment, Mr. Lessingham?" she persisted. "You must forgive my seeming inquisitive, but I am so interested in military affairs."

Lessingham bowed courteously.

"I do not remember alluding to my soldiering at all," he said coolly, "but as a matter of fact I am in the Guards."

Mrs. Johnson accepted Philippa's hand and the inevitable. Her good-by to Lessingham was most affable. She walked up the road with the vicar.

"I think, Vicar," she said severely, "that for a small place, Dreymarsh is becoming one of the worst centres of gossip I ever knew. Every one has been saying all sorts of unkind things about that charming Mr. Lessingham, and there you are—Major Felstead's friend and a Guardsman! Somehow or other, I felt that he belonged to one of the crack regiments. I shall certainly ask him to dinner one night next week."

The vicar nodded benignly. He had the utmost respect for Mrs. Johnson's cook, and his own standard of social desirability, to which the object of their discussion had attained.

"I should be happy to meet Mr. Lessingham at any time," he pronounced, with ample condescension. "I noticed him in church last Sunday morning."

CHAPTER XX

"My dear man, whatever shall I do with you!" Philippa exclaimed pathetically, as the door closed upon the last of her callers. "The Guards, indeed!"

Lessingham smiled as he resumed his place by her side.

"Well," he said, "I told the dear lady the truth. You will find my name well up in the list of the thirty-first battalion of the Prussian Guards."

She threw herself back in her chair and laughed. "How amusing it would be if it weren't all so terrible! You really are a perfect political Raffles. Do you know that this afternoon you have absolutely reestablished yourself? Mr. Johnson will probably call on you to-morrow—they may even ask you to dine—the vicar will write and ask for a subscription, and Dolly Fenwick will invite you to play golf with her."

"Do not turn my head," he begged.

"All the same," Philippa continued, more gravely, "I shall never have a moment's peace whilst you are in the place. I was thinking about you last night. I don't believe I have ever realised before how terrible it would be if you really were discovered. What would they do to you?"

"Whatever they might do," he replied, a little wearily, "I must obey orders. My orders are to remain here, but even if I were told that I might go, I should find it hard."

"Do you mean that?" she asked.

"I think you know," he answered.

"You men are so strange," she went on, after a moment's pause. "You give us so little time to know you, you show us so little of yourselves and you expect so much."

"We offer everything," he reminded her.

"I want to avoid platitudes," she said thoughtfully, "but is love quite the same thing for a man as for a woman?"

"Sometimes it is more," was the prompt reply. "Sometimes love, for a woman, means only shelter; often, for a man, love means the blending of all knowledge, of all beauty, all ambition, of all that he has learned from books and from life. Sometimes a man can see no further and needs to look no further."

Philippa suddenly felt that she was in danger. There was something in her heart of which she had never before been conscious, some music, some strange turn of sentiment in Lessingham's voice or the words themselves. It was madness, she told herself breathlessly. She was in love with her husband, if any one. She could not have lost all feeling for him so soon. She clasped her hands tightly. Lessingham seemed conscious of his advantage, and leaned towards her.

"If I were not offering you my whole life," he pleaded, "believe me, I would not open my lips. If I were thinking of episodes, I would throw myself into the sea before I asked you to give me even your fingers. But you, and you alone, could fill the place in my life which I have always prayed might be filled, not for a year or even a decade of years, but for eternity."

"Oh, but you forget!" she faltered.

"I remember so much," he replied, "that I know it is hard for you to speak. There are bonds which you have made sacred, and your fingers shrink from tearing them asunder. If it were not for this, Philippa—hear the speech of a renegade—my mandate should be torn in pieces. My instructions should flutter into the waste-paper basket, To-morrow should see us on our way to a new country and a new life. But you must be very sure indeed."

"Is it because of me that you are staying here?" she asked.

"Upon my honour, no," he assured her. "I must stay here a little longer, whatever it may mean for me. And so I am content to remain what I am to you at this minute. I ask from you only that you remain just what you are. But when the moment of my freedom comes, when my task here is finished and I turn to go, then I must come to you."

She rose suddenly to her feet, crossed the floor, and threw open the window. The breeze swept through the room, flapping the curtains, blowing about loose articles into a strange confusion. She stood there for several moments, as though in search of some respite from the emotional atmosphere upon which she had turned her back. When she finally closed the window, her hair was in little strands about her face. Her eyes were soft and her lips quivering.

"You make me feel," she said, taking his hand for a moment and looking at him almost piteously, "you make me feel everything except one thing."

"Except one thing?" he repeated.

"Can't you understand?" she continued, stretching out her hand with a quick, impulsive little movement. "I am here in Henry's house, his wife, the mistress of his household. All the years we've been married I have never thought of another man. I have never indulged in even the idlest flirtation. And now suddenly my life seems upside down. I feel as though, if Henry stood before me now, I would strike him on the cheek. I feel sore all over, and ashamed, but I don't know whether I have ceased to love him. I can't tell. Nothing seems to help me. I close my eyes and I try to think of that new world and that new life, and I know that there is nothing repulsive in it. I feel all the joy and the strength of being with you. And then there is Henry in the background. He seems to have had so much of my love."

He saw the tears gathering in her eyes, and he smiled at her encouragingly.

"Remember that at this moment I am asking you for nothing," he said. "Just think these things out. It isn't really a matter for sorrow," he continued. "Love must always mean happiness—for the one who is loved."

She leaned back in the corner of the sofa to which he had led her, her eyes dry now but still very soft and sweet. He sat by her side, fingering some of the things in her work basket. Once she held out her hand and seemed to find comfort in his clasp. He raised her fingers to his lips without any protest from her. She looked at him with a little smile.

"You know, I'm not at all an Ibsen heroine," she declared. "I can't see my way like those wonderful emancipated women."

"Yet," he said thoughtfully, "the way to the simple things is so clear."

Confidences were at an end for a time, broken up by the entrance of Nora and Helen, and some young men from the Depot, who had looked in for a game of billiards. Lessingham rose to leave as soon as the latter had returned to their game. His tone and manner now were completely changed. He seemed ill at ease and unhappy.

"I am going to have a day's fishing to-morrow," he told Philippa, "but I must admit that I have very little faith in this man Oates. They all tell me that your husband has any number of charts of the coast. Do you think I could borrow one?"

"Why, of course," she replied, "if we can find it."

She took him over to her husband's desk, opened such of the drawers as were not locked, and searched amongst their contents ruthlessly. By the time they had finished the last drawer, Lessingham had quite a little collection of charts, more or less finished, in his hand.

"I don't know where else to look," she said. "You might go through those and see if they are of any use. What is it, Mills?" she added, turning to the door.

Mills had entered noiselessly, and was watching the proceedings at Sir Henry's desk with a distinct lack of favour. He looked away towards his mistress, however, as he replied.

"The young woman has called with reference to a situation as parlour-maid, your ladyship," he announced. "I have shown her into the sewing room." Lady Cranston glanced at the clock.

"I sha'n't be more than five or ten minutes," she promised Lessingham. "Just look through those till I come back."

She hurried away, leaving Lessingham alone in the room. He stood for a moment listening. On the left-hand side, through the door which had been left ajar, he could hear the click of billiard balls and occasional peals of laughter. On the right-hand side there was silence. He moved swiftly across the room and closed the door leading into the billiard room, deposited on the sofa the charts which he had been carrying, and hurried back to the secretary. With a sickening feeling of overwhelming guilt, he drew from his pocket a key and opened, one by one, the drawers through which they had not searched. It took him barely five minutes to discover—nothing. With an air of relief he rearranged everything. When Philippa returned, he was sitting on the lounge, going through the charts which they had looked out together.

"Well?" she asked.

"There is nothing here," he decided, "which will help me very much. With your permission I will take this," he added, selecting one at random.

She nodded and they replaced the others. Then she touched him on the arm.

"Listen," she said, "are you perfectly certain that there is no one coming?"

He listened for a moment.

"I can't hear any one," he answered. "They've started a four-handed game of pool in the billiard room."

She smiled.

"Then I will disclose to you Henry's dramatic secret. See!"

She touched the spring in the side of the secretary. The false back, with its little collection of fishing flies, rolled slowly up. The large and very wonderful chart on which Sir Henry had bestowed so much of his time, was revealed. Lessingham gazed at it eagerly.

"There!" she said. "That has been a great labour of love with Henry. It is the chart, on a great scale, from which he works. I don't know a thing about it, and for heaven's sake never tell Henry that you have seen it."

He continued to examine the chart earnestly. Not a part of it escaped him. Then he turned back to Philippa.

"Is that supposed to be the coast on the other side of the point?" he asked.

"I don't exactly know where it is," she replied. "Every time Henry finds out anything new, he comes and works at it. I believe that very soon it will be perfect. Then he will start on another part of the coast."

"This is not the only one that he has prepared, then?" Lessingham enquired.

She shook her head.

"I believe it is the fifth," she replied. "They all disappear when they are finished, but I have no idea where to. To me they seem to represent a shocking waste of time."

Lessingham was suddenly taciturn. He held out his hand. "You are dining with us to-morrow night, remember," she said.

"I am not likely to forget," he assured her.

"And don't get drowned," she concluded. "I don't know any of these fishermen—I hate them all—but I'm told that Oates is the worst."

"I think that we shall be quite all right," he assured her. "Thanks very much for finding me the charts. What I have seen will help me."

Helen came in for a moment and their farewell was more or less perfunctory. Lessingham was almost thankful to escape. There was an unusual flush in his cheeks, a sense of bitter humiliation in his heart. All the fervour with which he had started on his perilous quest had faded away. No sense of duty or patriotism could revive his drooping spirits. He felt himself suddenly an unclean and dishonoured being.

CHAPTER XXI

Towards three o'clock on the following afternoon, the boisterous wind of an uncertain morning settled down to worse things. It tore the spray from the crest of the gathering waves, dashed it even against the French windows of Mainsail Haul, and came booming down the open spaces cliffwards, like the rumble of some subterranean artillery. A little group of fishermen in oilskins leaned over the railing and discussed the chances of Ben Oates bringing his boat in safely. Philippa, also, distracted by a curious anxiety, stood before the blurred window, gazing into what seemed almost a grey chaos.

"Captain Griffiths, your ladyship."

She turned around quickly at the announcement. Even an unwelcome caller at that moment was almost a relief to her.

"How nice of you to come and see me on such an afternoon, Captain Griffiths," she exclaimed, as they shook hands. "Helen is over at the Canteen, Nora is hard at work for once in her life, and I seem most dolefully alone."

Her visitor's reception of Philippa's greeting promised little in the way of enlivenment. He seemed more awkward and ill at ease than ever, and his tone was almost threatening.

"I am very glad to find you alone, Lady Cranston," he said. "I came specially to have a few words with you on a certain matter."

Her momentary impulse of relief at his visit passed away. There seemed to her something sinister in his manner. She was suddenly conscious that there was a new danger to be faced, and that this man's attitude towards her was, for some reason or other, inimical. After the first shock, however, she prepared herself to do battle.

"Well, you seem very mysterious," she observed. "I haven't broken any laws, have I? No lights flashing from any of my windows?"

"So far as I am aware, there are no complaints of the sort," the Commandant acknowledged, still speaking with an unnatural restraint. "My call, I hope, may be termed, to some extent, at least, a friendly one."

"How nice!" she sighed. "Then you'll have some tea, won't you?"

"Not at present, if you please," he begged. "I have come to talk to you about Mr. Hamar Lessingham."

"Really?" Philippa exclaimed. "Whatever has that poor man been doing now."

"Dreymarsh," her visitor proceeded, "having been constituted, during the last few months, a protected area, it is my duty to examine and enquire into the business of any stranger who appears here. Mr. Hamar Lessingham has been largely accepted without comment, owing to his friendship with you. I regret to state, however, that certain facts have come to my knowledge which make me wonder whether you yourself may not in some measure have been deceived."

"This sounds very ridiculous," Philippa interposed quietly.

"A few weeks ago," Captain Griffith continued, "we received information that this neighbourhood would probably be visited by some person connected with the Secret Service of Germany. There is strong evidence that the person in question is Mr. Hamar Lessingham."

"A graduate of Magdalen, my brother's intimate friend, and a frequent visitor at my father's house in Cheshire," Philippa observed, with faint sarcasm.

"The possibility of your having made a mistake, Lady Cranston," Captain Griffiths rejoined, "has, I must confess, only just occurred to me. The authorities at Magdalen College have been appealed to, and no one of the name of Lessingham was there during any one of your brother's terms."

Philippa took the blow well. She simply stared at her caller in a noncomprehending manner.

"We have also information," he continued gravely, "from Wood Norton Hall—from your mother, in fact, Lady Cranston—that no college friend of your brother, of that name, has ever visited Wood Norton."

"Go on," Philippa begged, a little faintly. "Did I ever live there myself? Was Richard ever at Magdalen?"

Captain Griffiths proceeded with the air of a man who has a task to finish and intends to do so, regardless of interruptions.

"I have had some conversation with Mr. Lessingham, in the course of which I asked him to explain his method of reaching here, and his last habitation. He simply fenced with me in the most barefaced fashion. He practically declined to give me any account of himself."

Philippa rose and rang the bell.

"I suppose I must give you some tea," she said, "although you seem to have come here on purpose to make my head ache."

"My object in coming here," Captain Griffiths rejoined, a little stiffly, "is to save you some measure of personal annoyance."

"Oh, please don't think that I am ungrateful," Philippa begged. "Of course, it is all some absurd mistake, and I'm sure we shall get to the bottom of it presently—Tell me what you think of the storm?" she added, as Mills entered with the tea tray. "Do you think it will get any worse, because I am terrified to death already?"

"I am no judge of the weather here," he confessed. "I believe the fishermen are preparing for something unusual."

She seated herself before the tea tray and insisted upon performing her duties as hostess. Afterwards she laid her hand upon his arm and addressed him with an air of complete candour.

"Now, Captain Griffiths," she began, "do listen to me. Just one moment of common sense, if you please. What do you suppose there could possibly be in our harmless seaside village to induce any one to risk his life by coming here on behalf of the Secret Service of Germany?"

"Dreymarsh," Captain Griffiths replied, "was not made a prohibited area for nothing."

"But, my dear man, be reasonable," Philippa persisted. "There are perhaps a thousand soldiers in the place, the usual preparations along the cliff for coast defence, a small battery of anti-aircraft guns, and a couple of searchlights. There isn't a grocer's boy in the place who doesn't know all this. There's no concealment about it. You must admit that Germany doesn't need to send over a Secret Service agent to acquaint herself with these insignificant facts."

Her visitor smiled very faintly. It was the first time he had relaxed even so far as this.

"I am not in possession of any information which I can impart to you, Lady Cranston," he said, "but I am not prepared to accept your statement that Dreymarsh contains nothing of greater interest than the things which you have mentioned."

There was no necessity for Philippa to play a part now. The suggestion contained in her visitor's words had really left her in a state of wonder.

"You are making my flesh creep!" she exclaimed. "You don't mean to say that we have secrets here?"

"I have said the last word which it is possible for me to say upon the subject," he declared. "You will understand, I am sure, that I am not here in the character of an inquisitor. I simply thought it my duty, in view of the fact that you had made yourself the social sponsor for Mr. Lessingham, to place certain information before you, and to ask, unofficially, of course, if you have any explanation to give? You may even," he went on, hesitatingly, "appreciate the motives which led me to do so."

"My dear man, what explanation could I have?" Philippa protested, "it is an absolute and undeniable fact that Mr. Lessingham was at Magdalen with my brother, and also that he visited us at Wood Norton. I know both these things of my own knowledge. The only possible explanation, therefore, is that you have been misinformed."

"Or," Captain Griffiths ventured, "that Mr. Hamar Lessingham in those days passed under another name."

"Another name?" Philippa faltered.

"Some such name, perhaps," he continued, "as Bertram Maderstrom."

There was a short silence. Captain Griffiths had leaned back in his chair and was caressing his upper lip. His eyes were fixed upon Philippa and Philippa saw nothing. Her little heel dug hard into the carpet. In a few seconds the room ceased to spin. Nevertheless, her voice sounded to her pitifully inadequate.

"What an absurdity all this is!" she exclaimed.

"Maderstrom," Captain Griffiths said thoughtfully, "was, curiously enough, an intimate college friend of your brother's. He was also a visitor at Wood Norton Hall. At neither place is there any trace of Mr. Hamar Lessingham. Perhaps you have made a mistake, Lady Cranston. Perhaps you have recognised the man and failed to remember his name. If so, now is the moment to declare it."

"I am very much obliged to you," Philippa retorted, "but I have never met or heard of this Mr. Maderstrom—"

"Baron Maderstrom," he interrupted.

"Baron Maderstrom, then, in my life; whereas Mr. Lessingham I remember perfectly."

"I am sorry," Captain Griffiths said, setting down his empty teacup and rising slowly to his feet. "We cannot help one another, then."

"If you want me to transfer Mr. Lessingham, whom I remember perfectly, into a German baron whom I never heard of," Philippa declared boldly, "I am afraid that we can't."

"Baron Maderstrom was a Swedish nobleman," Captain Griffiths observed.

"Swedish or German, I know nothing of him," Philippa persisted.

"There remains, then, nothing more to be said."

"I am afraid not," Philippa agreed sweetly.

"Under the circumstances," Captain Griffiths asked, "you will not, I am sure, expect me to dine to-night."

"Not if you object to meeting Mr. Hamar Lessingham," Philippa replied.

Her visitor's face suddenly darkened, and Philippa wondered vaguely whether anything more than professional suspicion was responsible for that little storm of passion which for a moment transformed his appearance. He quickly recovered, however.

"I may still," he concluded, moving towards the door, "be forced to present myself here in another capacity."

CHAPTER XXII

The confinement of the house, after the departure of her unwelcome visitor, stifled Philippa. Attired in a mackintosh, with a scarf around her head, she made her way on to the quay, and, clinging to the railing, dragged herself along to where the fishermen were gathered together in a little group. The storm as yet showed no signs of abatement.

"Has anything been heard of Ben Oates' boat?" she enquired.

An old fisherman pointed seawards.

"There she comes, ma'am, up on the crest of that wave; look!"

"Will she get in?" Philippa asked eagerly.

There were varied opinions, expressed in indistinct mutterings.

"She's weathering it grand," the fisherman to whom she had first spoken, declared. "We've a line ready yonder, and we're reckoning on getting 'em ashore all right. Lucky for Ben that the gentleman along with him is a fine sailor. Look at that, mum!" he added in excitement. "See the way he brought her head round to it, just in time. Boys, they'll come in on the next one!"

One by one the sailors made their way to the very edge of the wave-splashed beach. There were a few more minutes of breathless anxiety. Then, after the boat had disappeared completely from sight, hidden by a huge grey wall of sea, she seemed suddenly to climb to the top of it, to hover there, to become mixed up with the spray and the surf and a great green mass of waters, and then finally, with a harsh crash of timbers and a shout from the fishermen, to be flung high and dry upon the stones. Philippa, clutching the iron railing, saw for a moment nothing but chaos. Her knees became weak. She was unable to move. There was a queer dizziness in her ears. The sound of voices sounded like part of an unreal nightmare. Then she was aware of a single figure climbing the steps towards her. There was blood trickling down his face from the wound in the forehead, and he was limping slightly.

"Mr. Lessingham!" she called out, as he reached the topmost step. He took an eager step towards her.

"Philippa!" he exclaimed. "Why, what are you doing here?"

"I was frightened," she faltered. "Are you hurt?"

"Not in the least," he assured her. "We had a rough sail home, that's all, and that fellow Oates drank himself half unconscious. Come along, let me help you up the steps and out of this."

She clung to his arm, and they struggled up the private path to the house. Mills let them in with many expressions of concern, and Helen came hurrying to them from the background.

"I went out to see the storm," Philippa explained weakly, "and I saw Mr. Lessingham's boat brought in."

"And Mr. Lessingham will come this way at once," Helen insisted. "I haven't had a real case since I got my certificate, and I'm going to bind his head up."

Philippa began to feel her strength returning. The horror which lay behind those few minutes of nightmare rose up again in her mind. Mills had hurried on into the bathroom, and the other two were preparing to follow. She stopped them.

"Mr. Lessingham," she said, "listen. Captain Griffiths has been here. He knows or guesses everything."

"Everything?"

Philippa nodded.

"Helen must bind your head up, of course," she continued. "After that, think! What can we do? Captain Griffiths knows that there was no Hamar Lessingham at college with Dick, that he never visited Wood Norton, that there is some mystery about your arrival here, and he told me to my face that he believes you to be Bertram Maderstrom."

"What a meddlesome fellow!" Lessingham grumbled, holding his handkerchief to his forehead.

"Oh, please be serious!" Helen begged, looking up from the bandage which she was preparing. "This is horrible!"

"Don't I know it!" Philippa groaned. "Mr. Lessingham, you must please try and escape from here. You can have the car, if you like. There must be some place where you can go and hide until you can get away from the country."

"But I'm dining here to-night," Lessingham protested. "I'm not going to hide anywhere."

The two women exchanged glances of despair.

"Can't I make you understand!" Philippa exclaimed pathetically. "You're in danger here—really in danger!"

Lessingham's demeanour showed no appreciation of the situation.

"Of course, I can quite understand," he said, "that Griffiths is suspicious about me, but, after all, no one can prove that I have broken the law here, and I shall not make things any better by attempting an opera bouffe flight. Can I have my head tied up and come and talk to you about it later on?"

"Oh, if you like," Philippa assented weakly. "I can't argue."

She made her way up to her room and changed her wet clothes. When she came down, Lessingham was standing on the hearth rug in the library, with a piece of buttered toast in one hand and a cup of tea in the other. His head was very neatly bound up, and he seemed quite at his ease.

"You know," he began, as he wheeled a chair up to the fire for her, "that man Griffiths doesn't like me. He never took to me from the first, I could see that. If it comes to that, I don't like Griffiths. He is one of those mean, suspicious sort of characters we could very well do without."

Philippa, who had rehearsed a little speech several times in her bedroom, tried to be firm.

"Mr. Lessingham," she said, "you know that we are both your friends. Do listen, please. Captain Griffiths is Commandant here and in a position of authority. He has a very large power. I honestly believe that it is his intention to have you arrested—if not to-night, within a very few days."

"I do not see how he can," Lessingham objected, helping himself to another piece of toast. "I have committed no crime here. I have played golf with all the respectable old gentlemen in the place, and

I have given the committee some excellent advice as to the two new holes. I have played bridge down at the club—we will call it bridge!—and I have kept my temper like an angel. I have dined at Mess and told them at least a dozen new stories. I have kept my blinds drawn at night, and I have not a wireless secreted up the chimney. I really cannot see what they could do to me."

Philippa tried bluntness.

"You have served in the German army, and you are living in a protected area under a false name," she declared.

"Well, of course, there is some truth in what you say," he admitted, "but even if they have tumbled to that and can prove it, I should do no good by running away. To be perfectly serious," he added, setting his cup down, "there is only one thing at the present moment which would take me out of Dreymarsh, and that is if you believe that my presence here would further compromise you and Miss Fairclough."

Philippa was beginning to find her courage. "We're in it already, up to the neck," she observed. "I really don't see that anything matters so far as we are concerned."

"In that case," he decided, "I shall have the honour of presenting myself at the usual time."

CHAPTER XXIII

Philippa and Helen met in the drawing-room, a few minutes before eight that evening. Philippa was wearing a new black dress, a model of simplicity to the untutored eye, but full of that undefinable appeal to the mysterious which even the greatest artist frequently fails to create out of any form of colour. Some fancy had induced her to strip off her jewels at the last moment, and she wore no ornaments save a band of black velvet around her neck. Helen looked at her curiously.

"Is this a fresh scheme for conquest, Philippa?" she asked, as they stood together by the log fire.

Philippa unexpectedly flushed.

"I don't know what I was thinking about, really," she confessed. "Is that the exact time, I wonder?"

"Two minutes to eight," Helen replied.

"Mr. Lessingham is always so punctual," Philippa murmured. "I wonder if Captain Griffiths would dare!"

"We've done our best to warn him," Helen reminded her friend. "The man is simply pig-headed."

"I can't help feeling that he's right," Philippa declared, "when he argues that they couldn't really prove anything against him."

"Does that matter," Helen asked anxiously, "so long as he is an enemy, living under a false name here?"

"You don't think they'd—they'd—"

"Shoot him?" Helen whispered, lowering her voice. "They couldn't do that! They couldn't do that!"

The clock began to chime. Suddenly Philippa, who had been listening, gave a little exclamation of relief.

"I hear his voice!" she exclaimed. "Thank goodness!"

Helen's relief was almost as great as her companion's. A moment later Mills ushered in their guest. He was still wearing his bandage, but his colour had returned. He seemed, in fact, almost gay.

"Nothing has happened, then?" Philippa demanded anxiously, as soon as the door was closed.

"Nothing at all," he assured them. "Our friend Griffiths is terribly afraid of making a mistake."

"So afraid that he wouldn't come and dine. Never mind, you'll have to take care of us both," she added, as Mills announced dinner.

"I'll do my best," he promised, offering his arm.

If the sword of Damocles were indeed suspended over their heads, it seemed only to heighten the merriment of their little repast. Philippa had ordered champagne, and the warmth of the pleasant dining room, the many appurtenances of luxury by which they were surrounded, the glow of the wine, and the perfume of the hothouse flowers upon the table, seemed in delicious contrast to the fury of the storm outside. They all three appeared completely successful in a strenuous effort to dismiss all disconcerting subjects from their minds. Lessingham talked chiefly of the East. He had travelled in Russia, Persia, Afghanistan, and India, and he had the unusual but striking gift of painting little word pictures of some of the scenes of his wanderings. It was half-past nine before they rose from the table, and Lessingham accompanied them into the library. With the advent of coffee, they were for the first time really alone. Lessingham sat by Philippa's side, and Helen reclined in a low chair close at hand.

"I think," he said, "that I can venture now to tell you some news."

Helen put down her work. Philippa looked at him in silence, and her eyes seemed to dilate.

"I have hesitated to say anything about it," Lessingham went on, "because there is so much uncertainty about these things, but I believe that it is now finally arranged. I think that within the next week or ten days—perhaps a little before, perhaps a little later—your brother Richard will be set at liberty."

"Dick? Dick coming home?" Philippa cried, springing up from her reclining position.

"Dick?" Helen faltered, her work lying unheeded in her lap. "Mr. Lessingham, do you mean it? Is it possible?"

"It is not only possible," Lessingham assured them, "but I believe that it will come to pass. I have had to exercise a little duplicity, but I fancy that it has been successful. I have insisted that without help from an influential person in Dreymarsh, I cannot bring my labours here to a satisfactory conclusion, and I have named as the price of that help, Richard's absolute and immediate freedom. I heard only this morning that there would be no difficulty."

Helen snatched up her work and groped her way towards the door.

"I will come back in a few minutes," she promised, her voice a little broken.

Lessingham, who had opened the door for her, returned to his place. There were no tears in Philippa's brilliant eyes, but there was a faint patch of colour in her cheeks, and her lips were not quite steady. She caught at his hands.

"Oh, my dear, dear friend!" she said. "If only that little nightmare part of you did not exist. If only you could be just what you seem, and one could feel that you were there in our lives for always! I feel that I want to talk to you so much, to you and not the sham you. What shall I call you?"

"Bertram, please," he whispered.

"Then Bertram, dear," she went on, "for my sake, because you have really become dear to me, because my heart aches at the thought of your danger, and because—see how honest I am—I am a little afraid of myself—will you go away? The thought of your danger is like a nightmare to me. It all seems so absurd and unreasonable—I mean that the danger which I fear should be hanging over you. But I think that there is just a little something back of your brain of which you have never spoken, which it was your duty to keep to yourself, and it is just that something which brings the danger."

"I am not afraid for myself, Philippa," he told her. "I took a false step in life when I came here. What it was that attracted me I do not know. I think it was the thought of that wild ride amongst the clouds, and the starlight. It seemed such a wonderful beginning to any enterprise. And, Philippa, for one part of my adventure, the part which concerns you, it was a gorgeous prelude, and for the other— well, it just does not count because I have no fear. I have faith in my fortune, do you know that? I believe that I shall leave this place unharmed, but I believe that if I leave it without you, I shall go back to the worst hell in which a man could ever..."

"Bertram," she pleaded, "think of it all. Even if I cared enough—and I don't—there is something unnatural about it. Doesn't it strike you as horrible? My brother, my cousins, my father, are all fighting the men of the nation whose cause you have espoused! There is a horrible, eternal cloud of hatred which it will take generations to get rid of, if ever it disappears. How can we two speak of love! What part of the world could we creep into where people would not shrink away from us? I may have lost a little of my heart to you, Bertram, I may miss you when you go away, I may waste weary hours thinking, but that is all. Oh, you know that it must be all!"

"I do not," he answered stubbornly.

"Oh, you must be reasonable," she begged, with a little break in her voice. "You know very well that I ought not to listen to you. I ought not to welcome you here. I ought to be strong and close my ears."

"But you will not do that!"

"No!" she faltered. "Please don't come any nearer. I—"

She broke off suddenly. The struggle in her face was ended, her expression transformed. Her finger was held up as though to bid him listen. With her other hand she clutched the back of the couch. Her eyes were fixed upon the door. The little patch of wonderful colour faded from her cheeks.

"Listen!" she cried, with a note of terror in her voice. "That was the front door! Some one has come! Can't you hear them?"

Lessingham's hand stole suddenly to his pocket. She caught the glitter of something half withdrawn, and shrank back with a half-stifled moan.

"Not before you, dear," he promised. "Please do not be afraid. If this is the end, leave me alone with Griffiths. I shall not hurt him. I shall not forget. And if by any chance," he added, "this is to be our farewell, Philippa, you will remember that I love you as the flowers of the world love their sun. Courage!"

The door facing them was opened.

"Captain Griffiths," Mills announced.

Through the open door they caught a vision of two other soldiers and Inspector Fisher. Griffiths came into the room alone, however, and waited until the door was closed before he spoke. He carried himself as awkwardly as ever, but his long, lean face seemed to have taken to itself a new expression. He had the air of a man indulging in some strange pleasure.

"Lady Cranston," he said, "I am very sorry to intrude, but my visit here is official."

"What is it?" she asked hoarsely.

"I have received confirmatory evidence in the matter of which I spoke to you this afternoon," he went on. "I am sorry to disturb you at such an hour, but it is my duty to arrest this man on a charge of espionage."

Lessingham to all appearance remained unmoved.

"A most objectionable word," he remarked.

"A most villainous profession," Captain Griffiths retorted. "Thank heaven that in this country we are learning the art of dealing with its disciples."

"This is all a hideous mistake," Philippa declared feverishly. "I assure you that Mr. Lessingham has visited my father's house, that he was well-known to me years ago."

"As the Baron Maderstrom! What arguments he has used, Lady Cranston, to induce you to accept him here under his new identity, I do not know, but the facts are very clear."

"He seems quite convinced, doesn't he?" Lessingham remarked, turning to Philippa. "And as I gather that a portion of the British Army, assisted by the local constabulary, is waiting for me outside, perhaps I had better humour him."

"It would be as well, sir," Captain Griffiths assented grimly. "I am glad to find you in the humour for jesting."

Lessingham turned once more to Philippa. This time his tone was more serious.

"Lady Cranston," he begged, "won't you please leave us?"

"No!" she answered hysterically. "I know why you want me to, and I won't go! You have done no harm, and nothing shall happen to you. I will not leave the room, and you shall not—"

His gesture of appeal coincided with the sob in her throat. She broke down in her speech, and Captain Griffiths moved a step nearer.

"If you have any weapon in your possession, sir," he said, "you had better hand it over to me."

"Well, do you know," Lessingham replied, "I scarcely see the necessity. One thing I will promise you," he added, with a sudden flash in his eyes, "a single step nearer—a single step, mind—and you shall have as much of my weapon as will keep you quiet for the rest of your life. Remember that so long as you are reasonable I do not threaten you. Help me to persuade Lady Cranston to leave us."

Captain Griffiths was out of his depths. He was not a coward, but he had no hankering after death, and there was death in Lessingham's threat and in the flash of his eyes. While he hesitated, there was a knock upon the door. Mills came silently in. He carried a telegram upon a salver.

"For you, sir," he announced, addressing Captain Griffiths. "An orderly has just brought it down."

Griffiths looked at the pink envelope and frowned. He tore it open, however, without a word. As he read, his long, upper teeth closed in upon his lip. So he stood there until two little drops of blood appeared.

Then he turned to Mills.

"There is no answer," he said.

The man bowed and left the room. He walked slowly and he looked back from the doorway. It was scarcely possible for even so perfectly trained a servant to escape from the atmosphere of tragedy.

"Something tells me," Lessingham remarked coolly, as soon as the door was closed, "that that message concerns me."

The Commandant made no immediate reply. He straightened out the telegram and read it once more under the lamplight, as though to be sure there was no possible mistake. Then he folded it up and placed it in his waistcoat pocket.

"The notion of your arrest, sir," he said to Lessingham harshly, "is apparently distasteful to some one at headquarters who has not digested my information. I am withdrawing my men for the present."

"You're not going to arrest him?" Philippa cried.

"I am not," Captain Griffiths answered. "But," he added, turning to Lessingham, "this is only a respite. I have more evidence behind all that I have offered. You are Baron Bertram Maderstrom, a German spy, living here in a prohibited area under a false name. That I know, and that I shall prove to those who have interfered with me in the execution of my duty. This is not the end."

He left the room without even a word or a salute to Philippa. Lessingham looked after him for a moment, thoughtfully. Then he shrugged his shoulders.

"I am quite sure that I do not like Captain Griffiths," he declared. "There is no breeding about the fellow."

CHAPTER XXIV

Philippa, even for some moments after the departure of Captain Griffiths and his myrmidons, remained in a sort of nerveless trance. The crisis, with its bewildering denouement, had affected her curiously. Lessingham rose presently to his feet.

"I wonder," he asked, "if I could have a whisky and soda?"

She stamped her foot at him in a little fit of hysterical passion.

"You're not natural!" she cried. "Whisky and soda!"

"Well, I don't know," he protested mildly, helping himself from the table in the background. "I rather thought I was being particularly British. When in doubt, take a drink. That is Richard all the world over, you know."

She broke into a little mirthless laugh.

"I shall begin to think that you are a poseur!" she exclaimed.

He crossed the room towards her.

"Perhaps I am, dear," he confessed. "I want you just to sit up and lose that unnatural look. I am not really full of cheap bravado, but I am a philosopher. Something has happened to postpone—the end. Good luck to it, I say!"

He raised his tumbler to his lips and set it down empty. Philippa rose to her feet and walked restlessly to the window and back.

"I'll try and be reasonable too," she promised, resuming her seat. "I was right, you see. Captain Griffiths has discovered everything. Can you tell me what possible reason any one in London could have had for interference?"

"I seem to have got a friend up there without knowing it, don't I?" he observed.

"This is aging me terribly," Philippa declared, throwing herself back into her seat. "All my life I have hated mysteries. Here I am face to face with two absolutely insoluble ones. Captain Griffiths has assured me that there is here in Dreymarsh something of sufficient importance to account for the presence of a foreign spy. You have confirmed it. I have been torturing my brain about that for the last twenty-four hours. Now there happens something more inexplicable still. You are arrested, and you are not arrested. Your identity is known, and Captain Griffiths is forbidden to do his duty."

"It seems puzzling, does it not?" Lessingham agreed. "I shouldn't worry about the first, but this last little episode takes some explaining."

"If anything further happens this evening, I think I shall go mad," Philippa sighed.

"And something is going to happen," Lessingham declared, rising to his feet. "Did you hear that?"

Above even the roar of the wind they heard the brazen report of a gun from almost underneath the window. The room was suddenly lightened by a single vivid flash.

"A mortar!" Lessingham exclaimed. "And that was a rocket, unless I'm mistaken."

"The signal for the lifeboat!" Philippa announced. "I wonder if we can see anything."

She hastened towards the window, but paused at the abrupt opening of the door. Nora burst in, followed more sedately by Helen.

"Mummy, there's a wreck!" the former cried in excitement. "I heard something an hour ago, and I got up, and I've been sitting by the window, watching. I saw the lifeboat go out, and they're signalling now for the other one."

"It's quite true, Philippa," Helen declared. "We're going to try and fight our way down to the beach."

"I'll go, too," Lessingham decided. "Perhaps I may be of use."

"We'll all go," Philippa agreed. "Wait while I get my things on. What is it, Mills?" she added, as the door opened and the latter presented himself.

"There is a trawler on the rocks just off the breakwater, your ladyship," he announced. "They have just sent up from the beach to know if we can take some of the crew in. They are landing them as well as they can on the line."

"Of course we can," was the prompt reply. "Tell them to send as many as they want to. We will find room for them, somehow. I'll go upstairs and see about the fires. You'll all come back?" she added, turning around.

"We will all come back," Lessingham promised.

They fought their way down to the beach. At first the storm completely deafened all sound. The lanterns, waved here and there by unseen hands, seemed part of some ghostly tableau, of which the only background was the raging of the storm. Then suddenly, with a startling hiss, another rocket clove its way through the darkness. They had an instantaneous but brilliant view of all that was happening,— saw the trawler lying on its side, apparently only a few yards from the shore, saw the line stretched to the beach, on which, even at that moment, a man was being drawn ashore, licked by the spray, his strained face and wind-tossed hair clearly visible. Then all was darkness again more complete than ever. They struggled down on to the shingle, where the little cluster of fishermen were hard at work with the line. Almost the first person they ran across was Jimmy Dumble. He was standing on the edge of the breakwater with a great lantern in his hand, superintending the line, and, as they drew near, Lessingham, who was a little in advance, could hear his voice above the storm. He was shouting towards the wreck, his hand to his mouth.

"Send the master over next, you lubbers, or we'll cut the line. Do you hear?"

There was no reply or, if there was, it was drowned in the wind. Lessingham gripped the fisherman by the arm.

"Whom do you mean by 'master'?" he demanded. Dumble scarcely glanced at his interlocutor.

"Why, Sir Henry Cranston, to be sure," was the agitated answer. "These lubbers of sea hands are all coming off first, and the line won't stand for more than another one or two," he added, dropping his voice.

Then the thrill of those few minutes' excitement unrolled itself into a great drama before Lessingham's eyes. Sir Henry was on that ship as near as any man might wish to be to death.

"'Ere's the next," Jimmy muttered, as they turned the windlass vigorously. "Gosh, 'e's a heavy one, too!"

Then came a cry which sounded like a moan and above it the shrill fearful yell of a man who feels himself dropping out of the world's hearing. Lessingham raised the lantern which stood on the beach by Jimmy's side. The line had broken. The body of its suspended traveller had disappeared! And just then, strangely enough, for the first time for over an hour, the heavens opened in one great sheet of lightning, and they could see the figure of one man left on the ship, clinging desperately to the rigging.

"Tie the line around me," Jimmy shouted. "Let her go. Get the other end on the windlass."

They paid out the rope through their hands. Jimmy kicked off his boots and plunged into the cauldron. He swam barely a dozen strokes before he was caught on the top of an incoming wave, tossed about like a cork and flung back upon the beach, where he lay groaning. There was a little murmur amongst the fisherman, who rushed to lean over him.

"Swimming ain't no more use than trying to walk on the water," one of them declared.

Lessingham raised the lantern which he was carrying, and flashed it around.

"Where are the young ladies?" he asked.

"Gone up to the house with two as we've just taken off the wreck," some one informed him.

Lessingham stooped down. Willing hands helped him unfasten the cord from Jimmy's waist. He tore off his own coat and waistcoat and boots. Some helped, other sought to dissuade him, as he secured the line around his own waist.

"We've sent for more rockets," one man shouted in his ear. "The man will be back in half an hour."

Lessingham pushed them on one side. He stood on the edge of the beach and, borrowing a lantern, watched for his opportunity. Then suddenly he vanished. They looked after him. They could see nothing but the rope slipping past their feet, inch by inch. Sometimes it was stationary, sometimes it was drawn taut. The first great wave that came flung a yard or so of slack amongst them. Then, after the roar of its breaking had died away, they saw the rope suddenly tighten, and pass rapidly out, and the excitement began to thicken.

"That 'un didn't get him, anyway," one of them muttered.

"He'll go through the next, with luck," another declared hopefully.

Lessingham, fighting for his consciousness, deafened and half stunned by the roar of the waters about him, still felt the exhilaration of that great struggle. He looked once into seas which seemed to touch the clouds, drew himself stiff, and plunged into the depths of a mountain of foaming waters, whose summit seemed to him like one of those grotesque and nightmare-distorted efforts of the opium-eating brain. Then the roar sounded all behind him, and he knew that he was through the breakers. He swam to the side of the ship and clutched hold of a chain. It was Sir Henry's out-stretched hand which pulled him on to the deck.

"My God, that was a swim!" the latter declared, as he pulled his rescuer up, not in the least recognising him. "Let's have the end of that cord, quick! So!" he went on, paying it out through his fingers until the end of the rope appeared. "You'd better get your breath, young man, and then over you go. I'll follow."

"I'm damned if I do!" was the vigorous reply. "You start off while I get my breath."

They were suddenly half drowned with a shower of spray. Sir Henry held Lessingham in a grip of iron, or he would have been swept overboard.

"Get one arm through the chains, man," he shouted. "My God!" he added, peering through the gloom. "Lessingham!"

"Well, don't stop to worry about that," was the fierce reply. "Let's get on with our job."

Sir Henry threw off his oilskins and his underneath coat.

"Follow me when they wave the lantern twice," he directed. "If we either of us get the knock—well, thanks!"

Lessingham felt the grip of Sir Henry's hand as he passed him and went overboard into the darkness. Then, with one arm through the chains, he drew towards him by means of his heel the coat which Sir Henry had thrown upon the deck. Gradually it came within reach of his disengaged hand. He seized it, shook it out, and dived eagerly into the breast pocket. There were several small articles which he threw ruthlessly away, and then a square packet, wrapped in oilcloth, which bent to his fingers. Another breaking wave threw him on his back. One arm was still through the chain, the other gripped what some illuminating instinct had already convinced him was the chart! As soon as he had recovered his breath, a grim effort of humour parted his lips. He lay there for a moment and laughed till the spray, this time with a rush of green water underneath, very nearly swept him from his place.

They were waving a lantern on the beach when he struggled again to his feet.

He slipped the little packet down his clothes next to his skin, and groped about to find the end of the line which Sir Henry and he had fastened to a staple below the chains. Then he drew a long breath, gripped the rope and shouted. A second or two later he was back in the cauldron.

As they pulled him on to the beach, he had but one idea. Whatever happened, he must not lose consciousness. The packet was still there against the calf of his leg. It must be his own hands which removed his clothes. It seemed to him that those few bronzed faces, those half a dozen rude lanterns, had become magnified and multiplied a hundredfold. It was an army of blue-jerseyed fishermen which patted him on the back and welcomed him, lanterns like the stars flashing everywhere around. He set his teeth and fought against the buzzing in his ears. He tried to speak, and his voice sounded like a weak, far away whisper.

"I am all right," he kept on saying.

Then he felt himself leaning on two brawny arms. His feet followed the mesmeric influence of their movement. Was he going into the clouds, he wondered? They stopped to open a gate, the gate leading to the gardens of Mainsail Haul. How did he get there? He had no idea. More movements of his feet, and then unexpected warmth. He looked around him. There were voices. He listened. The one voice? The one face bending over his, her eyes wet with tears, her whispers an incoherent stream of broken words. Then the warmth seemed to come back to his veins. He sat up and found himself on the couch in the library, the rain dripping from him in little pools, and he knew that he had succeeded. He had not fainted.

"I am all right," he repeated. "What a mess I am making!"

The voices around him were still a little tangled, but the hand which held a steaming tumbler to his lips was Philippa's.

"Drink it all," she begged.

He felt the tears come into his eyes, felt the warm blood streaming through his body, felt a little wet patch at the back of the calf of his leg, and the hand which set down the empty tumbler was almost steady.

"There's a hot bath ready," Philippa told him; "some dry clothes, and a bedroom with a fire in. Do let Mills show you the way."

He rose at once, prepared to follow her. His feet were not quite so steady as he would have wished, but he made a very presentable show. Mills, with a little apology, held out his arm. Philippa walked by his other side.

"As soon as you have finished your bath and got into some dry clothes," Philippa whispered, "please ring, or send Mills to let us know."

He was even able to smile at her.

"I am quite all right," he assured her once more.

CHAPTER XXV

Philippa, unusually early on the following morning, glanced at the empty breakfast table with a little air of disappointment, and rang the bell.

"Mills," she enquired, "is no one down?"

"Sir Henry is, I believe, on the beach, your ladyship," the man answered, "and Miss Helen and Miss Nora are with him."

"And Mr. Lessingham?"

"Mr. Lessingham, your ladyship," Mills continued, looking carefully behind him as though to be sure that the door was closed, "has disappeared."

"Disappeared?" Philippa repeated. "What do you mean, Mills?"

"I left Mr. Lessingham last night, your ladyship," Mills explained, "in a suit of the master's clothes and apparently preparing for bed—I should say this morning, as it was probably about two o'clock. I called him at half past eight, as desired, and found the room empty. The bed had not been slept in."

"Was there no note or message?" Philippa asked incredulously.

"Nothing, your ladyship. One of the maid servants believes that she heard the front door open at five o'clock this morning."

"Ring up the hotel," Philippa instructed, "and see if he is there."

Mills departed to execute his commission. Philippa stood looking out of the window, across the lawn and shrubbery and down on to the beach. There was still a heavy sea, but it was merely the swell from the day before. The wind had dropped, and the sun was shining brilliantly. Sir Henry, Helen, and Nora were strolling about the beach as though searching for something. About fifty yards out, the wrecked trawler was lying completely on its side, with the end of one funnel visible. Scattered groups of the villagers were examining it from the sands. In due course Mills returned.

"The hotel people know nothing of Mr. Lessingham, your ladyship, beyond the fact that he did not return last night. They received a message from Hill's Garage, however, about half an hour ago, to say that their mechanic had driven Mr. Lessingham early this morning to Norwich, where he had caught the mail train to London, The boy was to say that Mr. Lessingham would be back in a day or so."

Philippa pushed open the windows and made her way down towards the beach. She leaned over the rail of the promenade and waved her hand to the others, who clambered up the shingle to meet her.

"Scarcely seen you yet, my dear, have I?" Sir Henry observed.

He stooped and kissed her forehead, a salute which she suffered without response. Helen pointed to the wreck.

"It doesn't seem possible, does it," she said, "that men's lives should have been lost in that little space. Two men were drowned, they say, through the breaking of the rope. They recovered the bodies this morning."

"Everything else seems to have been washed on shore except my coat," Sir Henry grumbled. "I was down here at daylight, looking for it."

"Your coat!" Philippa repeated scornfully. "Fancy thinking of that, when you only just escaped with your life!"

"But to tell you the truth, my dear," Sir Henry explained, "my pocketbook and papers of some value were in the pocket of that coat. I can't think how I came to forget them. I think it was the surprise of seeing that fellow Lessingham crawl on to the wreck looking like a drowned rat. Jove, what a pluck he must have!"

"The fishermen can talk of nothing else," Nora put in excitedly. "Mummy, it was simply splendid! Helen and I had gone up with two of the rescued men, but I got back just in time to see them fasten the rope round his waist and watch him plunge in."

"How is he this morning?" Helen asked.

"Gone," Philippa replied.

They all looked at her in surprise.

"Gone?" Sir Henry repeated. "What, back to the hotel, do you mean?"

"His bed has not been slept in," Philippa told them. "He must have slipped away early this morning, gone to Hill's Garage, hired a car, and motored to Norwich. From there he went on to London. He has sent word that he will be back in a few days."

"I hope to God he won't!" Sir Henry muttered.

Philippa swung round upon him.

"What do you mean by that?" she demanded. "Don't you want to thank him for saving your life?"

"My dear, I certainly do," Sir Henry replied, "but just now—well, I am a little taken aback. Gone to London, eh? Tore away without warning in the middle of the night to London! And coming back, too—that's the strange part of it!"

One would think, from Sir Henry's expression, that he was finding food for much satisfaction in this recital of Lessingham's sudden disappearance.

"He is a wonderful fellow, this Lessingham," he added thoughtfully. "He must have—yes, by God, he must have—In that storm, too!"

"If you could speak coherently, Henry," Philippa observed, "I should like to say that I am exceedingly anxious to know why Mr. Lessingham has deserted us so precipitately."

Sir Henry would have taken his wife's arm, but she avoided him. He shrugged his shoulders and plodded up the steep path by her side.

"The whole question of Lessingham is rather a problem," he said. "Of course, you and Helen have seen very much more of him than I have. Isn't it true that people have begun to make curious remarks about him?"

"How did you know that, Henry?" Philippa demanded.

"Well, one hears things," he replied. "I should gather, from what I heard, that his position here had become a little precarious. Hence his sudden disappearance."

"But he is coming back again," Philippa reminded her husband.

"Perhaps!"

Philippa signified her desire that her husband should remain a little behind with her. They walked side by side up the gravel path. Philippa kept her hands clasped behind her.

"To leave the subject of Mr. Lessingham for a time," she began, "I feel very reluctant to ask for explanations of anything you do, but I must confess to a certain curiosity as to why I should find you lunching at the Canton with two very beautiful ladies, a few days ago, when you left here with Jimmy Dumble to fish for whiting; and also why you return here on a trawler which belongs to another part of the coast?"

Sir Henry made a grimace.

"I was beginning to wonder whether curiosity was dead," he observed good-humouredly. "If you wouldn't mind giving me another—well, to be on the safe side let us say eight days—I think I shall be able to offer you an explanation which you will consider satisfactory."

"Thank you," Philippa rejoined, with cold surprise; "I see no reason why you should not answer such simple questions at once."

Sir Henry sighed deprecatingly, and made another vain attempt to take his wife's arm.

"Philippa, be a little brick," he begged. "I know I seem to have been playing the part of a fool just lately, but there has been a sort of reason for it."

"What reason could there possibly be," she demanded, "which you could not confide in me?"

He was silent for a moment. When he spoke again there was a new earnestness in his tone.

"Philippa," he said, "I have been working for some time at a little scheme which isn't ripe to talk about yet, not even to you, but which may lead to something which I hope will alter your opinion. You couldn't see your way clear to trust me a little longer, could you?" he begged, with rather a plaintive gleam in his blue eyes. "It would make it so much easier for me to say no more but just have you sit tight."

"I wonder," she answered coldly, "if you realise how much I have suffered, sitting tight, as you call it, and waiting for you to do something!"

"My fishing excursions," he went on desperately, "have not been altogether a matter of sport."

"I know that quite well," she replied. "You have been making that chart you promised your miserable fishermen. None of those things interest me, Henry. I fear—I am very much inclined to say that none of your doings interest me. Least of all," she went on, her voice quivering with passion, "do I appreciate in the least these mysterious appeals for my patience. I have some common sense, Henry."

"You're a suspicious little beast," he told her.

"Suspicious!" she scoffed. "What a word to use from a man who goes off fishing for whiting, and is lunching at the Carlton, some days afterwards, with two ladies of extraordinary attractions!"

"That was a trifle awkward," Sir Henry admitted, with a little burst of candour, "but it goes in with the rest, Philippa."

"Then it can stay with the rest," she retorted, "exactly where I have placed it in my mind. Please understand me. Your conduct for the last twelve months absolves me from any tie there may be between us. If this explanation that you promise comes—in time, and I feel like it, very well. Until it does, I am perfectly free, and you, as my husband, are non-existent. That is my reply, Henry, to your request for further indulgence."

"Rather a foolish one, my dear," he answered, patting her shoulder, "but then you are rather a child, aren't you?"

She swung away from him angrily.

"Don't touch me!" she exclaimed. "I mean every word of what I have said. As for my being a child—well, you may be sorry some day that you have persisted in treating me like one."

Sir Henry paused for a moment, watching her disappearing figure. There was an unusual shade of trouble in his face. His love for and confidence in his wife had been so absolute that even her threats had seemed to him like little morsels of wounded vanity thrown to him out of the froth of her temper. Yet at that moment a darker thought crossed his mind. Lessingham, he realised, was not a rival, after all, to be despised. He was a man of courage and tact, even though Sir Henry, in his own mind, had labelled him as a fool. If indeed he were coming back to Dreymarsh, what could it be for? How much had Philippa known about him? He stood there for a few moments in indecision.

A great impulse had come to him to break his pledge, to tell her the truth. Then he made his disturbed way into the breakfast room.

"Where's your mother, Nora?" he asked, as Helen took Philippa's place at the head of the table.

"She wants some coffee and toast sent up to her room." Nora explained. "The wind made her giddy."

Sir Henry breakfasted in silence, rang the bell, and ordered his car.

"You going away again, Daddy?" Nora asked.

"I am going to London this morning," he replied, a little absently.

"To London?" Helen repeated. "Does Philippa know?"

"I haven't told her yet."

Helen turned towards Nora.

"I wish you'd run up and see if your mother wants any more coffee, there's a dear," she suggested.

Nora acquiesced at once. As soon as she had left the room, Helen leaned over and laid her hand upon Sir Henry's arm.

"Don't go to London, Henry," she begged.

"But my dear Helen, I must," he replied, a little curtly.

"I wouldn't if I were you," she persisted. "You know, you've tried Philippa very high lately, and she is in an extremely emotional state. She is all worked up about last night, and I wouldn't leave her alone if I were you."

Sir Henry's blue eyes seemed suddenly like points of steel as he leaned towards her.

"You think that she is in love with that fellow Lessingham?" he asked bluntly.

"No, I don't," Helen replied, "but I think she is more furious with you than you believe. For months you have acted—well, how shall I say?"

"Oh, like a coward, if you like, or a fool. Go on."

"She has asked for explanations to which she is perfectly entitled," Helen continued, "and you have given her none. You have treated her like something between a doll and a child. Philippa is as good and sweet as any woman who ever lived, but hasn't it ever occurred to you that women are rather mysterious beings? They may sometimes do, out of a furious sense of being wrongly treated, out of a sort of aggravated pique, what they would never do for any other reason. If you must go, come back to-night, Henry. Come back, and if you are obstinate, and won't tell Philippa all that she has a right to know, tell her about that luncheon in town."

Sir Henry frowned.

"It's all very well, you know, Helen," he said, "but a woman ought to trust her husband."

"I am your friend, remember," Helen replied, "and upon my word, I couldn't trust and believe even in Dick, if he behaved as you have done for the last twelve months."

Sir Henry made a grimace.

"Well, that settles it, I suppose, then," he observed. "I'll have one more try and see what I can do with Philippa. Perhaps a hint of what's going on may satisfy her."

He climbed the stairs, meeting Nora on her way down, and knocked at his wife's door. There was no reply. He tried the handle and found the door locked.

"Are you there, Philippa?" he asked.

"Yes!" she replied coldly.

"I am going to London this morning. Can I have a few words with you first?"

"No!"

Sir Henry was a little taken aback.

"Don't be silly, Philippa," he persisted. "I may be away for four or five days."

There was no answer. Sir Henry suddenly remembered another entrance from a newly added bathroom. He availed himself of it and found Philippa seated in an easy-chair, calmly progressing with her breakfast. She raised her eyebrows at his entrance.

"These are my apartments," she reminded him.

"Don't be a little fool," he exclaimed impatiently.

Philippa deliberately buttered herself a piece of toast, picked up her book, and became at once immersed in it.

"You don't wish to talk to me, then?" he demanded.

"I do not," she agreed. "You have had all the opportunities which any man should need, of explaining certain matters to me. My curiosity in them has ended; also my interest—in you. You say you are going to London. Very well. Pray do not hurry home on my account."

Sir Henry, as he turned to leave the room, made the common mistake of a man arguing with a woman—he attempted to have the last word.

"Perhaps I am better out of the way, eh?"

"Perhaps so," Philippa assented sweetly.

CHAPTER XXVI

Philippa, late that afternoon, found what she sought—solitude. She had walked along the sands until Dreymarsh lay out of sight on the other side of a spur of the cliffs. Before her stretched a long and level plain, a fringe of sand, and a belt of shingly beach. There was not a sign of any human being in sight, and of buildings only a quaint tower on the far horizon.

She found a dry place on the pebbles, removed her hat and sat down, her hands clasped around her knees, her eyes turned seaward. She had come out here to think, but it was odd how fugitive and transient her thoughts became. Her husband was always there in the background, but in those moments it was Lessingham who was the predominant figure. She remembered his earnestness, his tender solicitude for her, the courage which, when necessity demanded, had flamed up in him, a born and natural quality. She remembered the agony of those few minutes on the preceding day, when nothing but what still seemed a miracle had saved him. At one moment she felt herself inclined to pray that he might never come back. At another, her heart ached to see him once more. She knew so well that if he came it would be for her sake, that he would come to ask her finally the question with which she had fenced. She knew, too, that his coming would be the moment of her life. She was so much of a woman, and the passionate craving of her sex to give love for love was there in her heart, almost omnipotent. And in the background there was that bitter desire to bring suffering upon the man who had treated her like a child, who had placed her in a false position with all other women, who had dawdled and idled away his days, heedless of his duty, heedless of every serious obligation. When she tried to reason, her way seemed so clear, and yet, behind it all, there was that cold impulse of almost Victorian prudishness, the inheritance of a long line of virtuous women, a prudishness which she had once, when she had believed that it was part of her second nature, scoffed at as being the outcome of one of the finer forms of selfishness.

She told herself that she had come there to decide, and decision came no nearer to her. A late afternoon star shone weakly in the sky. A faint, vaporous mist obscured the horizon and floated in tangled wreaths upon the face of the sea. Only that line of sand seemed still clear-cut and distinct, and as she glanced along it her eyes were held by something approaching, something which seemed at first nothing but a black, moving speck, then gradually resolved itself into the semblance of a man on horseback, galloping furiously. She watched him as he drew nearer and nearer, the sand flying from his horse's hoofs, his figure motionless, his eyes apparently fixed upon some distant spot. It was not until he had come within fifty yards of her that she recognised him. His horse shied at the sight of her and was suddenly swung round with a powerful wrist. Little specks of sand, churned up in the momentary stampede of hoofs, fell upon her skirt. For the rest, she watched the struggle composedly, a struggle which was over almost as soon as it was begun. Captain Griffiths leaned down from his trembling but subdued horse.

"Lady Cranston!" he exclaimed in astonishment.

"That's me," she replied, smiling up at him. "Have you been riding off your bad temper?"

He glanced down at his horse's quivering sides. Back as far as one could see there was that regular line of hoof marks.

"Am I bad-tempered?" he asked.

"Well," she observed, "I don't know you well enough to answer that question. I was simply thinking of yesterday evening."

He slipped from his horse and stood before her. His long, severe face had seldom seemed more malevolent.

"I had enough to make me bad-tempered," he declared. "I had tracked down a German spy, step by step, until I had him there, waiting for arrest—expecting it, even—and then I got that wicked message."

"What was that wicked message after all?" she enquired.

"That doesn't matter," he answered. "It was from a quarter where they ought to know better, and it ordered me to make no arrest. I have sent to the War Office to-day a full report, and I am praying that they may change their minds."

Philippa sighed.

"If you hadn't received that telegram last night," she observed, "it seems to me that I should have been a widow to-day."

He frowned, and struck his boot heavily with his riding whip.

"Yes, I heard of that," he admitted. "I dare say if he hadn't gone, though, some one else would."

"Would you have gone if you had been there?" she asked.

"If you had told me to," he replied, looking at her steadfastly.

Philippa felt a little shiver. There was something ominous in the intensity of his gaze and the meaning which he had contrived to impart to his tone. She rose to her feet.

"Well," she said, "don't let me keep you here. I am getting cold."

He passed his arm through the bridle of his horse. "I will walk with you, if I may," he proposed. She made no reply, and they set their faces homewards.

"I hear Lessingham has left the place," he remarked, a little abruptly.

"Oh, I expect he'll come back," Philippa replied.

"How long is it, Lady Cranston, since you took to consorting with German spies?" he asked.

"Don't be foolish—or impertinent," she enjoined. "You are making a ridiculous mistake about Mr. Lessingham."

He laughed unpleasantly.

"No need for us to fence," he said. "You and I know who he is. What I do want to know, what I have been wondering all the way from the point there—four miles of hard galloping and one question—why are you his friend? What is he to you?"

"Really, Captain Griffiths," she protested, looking up at him, "of what possible interest can that be to you?"

"Well, it is, anyhow," he answered gruffly. "Anything that concerns you is of interest to me."

Philippa realised at that moment, perhaps for the first time, what it all meant. She realised the significance of those apparently purposeless afternoon calls, when through sheer boredom she had had to send for Helen to help her out; the significance of those long silences, the melancholy eyes which seemed to follow her movements. She felt an unaccountable desire to laugh, and then, at the first twitchings of her lips, she restrained herself. She knew that tragedy was stalking by her side.

"I think, Captain Griffiths," she said gravely, "that you are talking nonsense, and you are not a very good hand at it. Won't you please ride on?"

He made no movement to mount his horse. He plodded along the soft sand by her side—a queer, elongated figure, his gloomy eyes fixed upon the ground.

"Until this fellow Lessingham came you were never so hard," he persisted.

She looked at him with genuine curiosity.

"I was never so hard?" she repeated. "Do you imagine that I have ever for a single moment considered my demeanour towards you—you of all persons in the world? I simply don't remember when you have been there and when you haven't. I don't remember the humours in which I have been when we have conversed. All that you have said seems to me to be the most arrant nonsense."

He swung himself into the saddle and gathered up the reins.

"Thank you," he said bitterly, "I understand. Only let me tell you this," he went on, his whip poised in his hand. "You may have powerful friends who saved your—"

He hesitated so long that she glanced up at him and read all that he had wished to say in his face.

"My what?" she asked.

His courage failed him.

"Mr. Lessingham," he proceeded, "from arrest. But if he shows his face here again in Dreymarsh, I sha'n't stop to arrest him. I shall shoot him on sight and chance the consequences."

"They'll hang you!" she declared savagely.

He laughed at her.

"Hang me for shooting a man whom I can prove to be a German spy? They won't dare! They won't even dare to place me under arrest for an hour. Why, when the truth becomes known," he went on, his voice gaining courage as the justice of his case impressed itself upon him, "what do you suppose is going to happen to two women who took this fellow in and befriended him, introduced him under a false name to their friends, gave him the run of their house—this man whom they knew all the time was a German? You, Lady Cranston, chafing and scolding your husband by night and by day because he isn't where you think he ought to be; you, so patriotic that you cannot bear the sight of him out of uniform; you—the hostess, the befriender, the God knows what of Bertram Maderstrom! It will be a pretty tale when it's all told!"

"I really think," Philippa asserted calmly, "that you are the most utterly impossible and obnoxious creature I have ever met."

His face was dangerous for a moment. They had not yet reached the promontory which sheltered them from Dreymarsh.

"Perhaps," he muttered, leaning malignly towards her, "I could make myself even more obnoxious."

"Quite possibly," she replied, "only I want to tell you this. If you come a single inch nearer to me, one of them shall shoot you."

"Your friend or your husband, eh?" he scoffed.

She waved him on.

"I think," she told him, "that either of them would be quite capable of ridding the world of a coward like you."

"A coward?" he repeated.

"Precisely! Isn't it a coward's part to terrorise a woman?"

"I don't want to terrorise you," he said sulkily.

"Well, you must admit that you haven't shown any particular desire to make yourself agreeable," she pointed out.

He turned suddenly upon her.

"I am a fool, I know," he declared bitterly. "I'm an awkward, nervous, miserable fool, my own worst enemy as they say of me in the Mess, turning the people against me I want to have like me, stumbling into every blunder a fool can. I'm the sort of man women make sport of, and you've done it for them cruelly, perfectly."

"Captain Griffiths!" she protested. "When have I ever been anything but kind and courteous to you?"

"It isn't your kindness I want, nor your courtesy! There's a curse upon my tongue," he went on desperately. "I'm not like other men. I don't know how to say what I feel. I can't put it into words. Every one misunderstands me. You, too! Here I rode up to you this afternoon and my heart was beating for joy, and in five minutes I had made an enemy of you. Damn that fellow Lessingham! It is all his fault!"

Without the slightest warning he brought down his hunting crop upon his horse's flanks. The mare gave one great plunge, and he was off, riding at a furious gallop. Philippa watched him with immense relief. In the far distance she could see two little specks growing larger and larger. She hurried on towards them.

"Whatever did you do to Captain Griffiths, Mummy?" Nora demanded. "Why he passed us without looking down, galloping like a madman, and his face looked—well, what did it look like, Helen?"

Helen was gazing uneasily along the sands.

"Like a man riding for his enemy," she declared.

CHAPTER XXVII

Philippa and Helen looked at one another a little dolefully across the luncheon table.

"I suppose one misses the child," Helen said.

"I feel too depressed for words," Philippa admitted.

"A few days ago," Helen reminded her companion, "we were getting all the excitement that was good for any one."

"And a little more," Philippa agreed. "I don't know why things seem so flat now. We really ought to be glad that nothing terrible has happened."

"What with Henry and Mr. Lessingham both away," Helen continued, "and Captain Griffiths not coming near the place, we really have reverted to the normal, haven't we? I wonder—if Mr. Lessingham has gone back."

"I do not think so," Philippa murmured.

Helen frowned slightly.

"Personally," she said, with some emphasis, "I hope that he has."

"If we are considering the personal point of view only," Philippa retorted, "I hope that he has not."

Helen looked her disapproval.

"I should have thought that you had had enough playing with fire," she observed.

"One never has until one has burned one's fingers," Philippa sighed. "I know perfectly well what is the matter with you," she continued severely. "You are fretting because curried chicken is Dick's favourite dish."

"I am not such a baby," Helen protested. "All the same, it does make one think. I wonder—"

"I know exactly what you were going to say," Philippa interrupted. "You were going to say that you wondered whether Mr. Lessingham would keep his promise."

"Whether he would be able to," Helen corrected. "It does seem so impossible, doesn't it?"

"So does Mr. Lessingham himself," Philippa reminded her. "It isn't exactly a usual thing, is it, to have a perfectly charming and well-bred young man step out of a Zeppelin into your drawing-room."

"You really believe, then," Helen asked eagerly, "that he will be able to keep his promise?"

Philippa nodded confidently.

"Do you know," she said, "I believe that Mr. Lessingham, by some means or another, would keep any promise he ever made. I am expecting to see Dick at any moment now, so you can get on with your lunch, dear, and not sit looking at the curry with tears in your eyes."

"It isn't the curry so much as the chutney," Helen protested faintly. "He never would touch any other sort."

"Well, I shouldn't be surprised if he were here to finish the bottle," Philippa declared. "I have a feeling this morning that something is going to happen."

"How long has Nora gone away for?" Helen enquired, after a moment's pause.

"A fortnight or three weeks," Philippa answered. "Her grandmother wired that she would be glad to have her until Christmas."

"Just why," Helen asked seriously, "have you sent her away?"

Philippa toyed with her curry, and glanced around as though she regretted Mills' absence from the room.

"I thought it best," she said quietly. "You see, I am not quite sure what the immediate future of this menage is going to be."

Helen leaned across the table and laid her hand upon her friend's.

"Dear," she sighed, "it worries me so to hear you talk like that."

"Why?"

"Because you know perfectly well, although you profess to ignore it, that at the bottom of your heart there is no one else but Henry. It isn't fair, you know."

"To whom isn't it fair?" Philippa demanded.

"To Mr. Lessingham."

Philippa was thoughtful for a few moments.

"Perhaps," she admitted, "that is a point of view which I have not sufficiently considered."

Helen pressed home her advantage.

"I don't think you realise, Philippa," she said, "how madly in love with you the man is. In a perfectly ingenuous way, too. No one could help seeing it."

"Then where does the unfairness come in?" Philippa asked. "It is within my power to give him all that he wants."

"But you wouldn't do it, Philippa. You know that you wouldn't!" Helen objected. "You may play with the idea in your mind, but that's just as far as you'd ever get."

Philippa looked her friend steadily in the face. "I disagree with you, Helen," she said. Helen set down the glass which she had been in the act of raising to her lips. It was her first really serious intimation of the tragedy which hovered over her future sister-in-law's life. Somehow or other, Philippa had seemed, even to her, so far removed from that strenuous world of over-drugged, over-excited feminine decadence, to whom the changing of a husband or a lover is merely an incident in the day's excitements. Philippa, with her frail and almost flowerlike beauty, her love of the wholesome ways of life, and her strong affections, represented other things. Now, for the first time, Helen was really afraid, afraid for her friend.

"But you couldn't ever—you wouldn't leave Henry!"

Philippa seemed to find nothing monstrous in the idea.

"That is just what I am seriously thinking of doing," she confided.

Helen affected to laugh, but her mirth was obviously forced. Their conversation ceased perforce with the return of Mills into the room.

Then the wonderful thing happened. The windows of the dining room faced the drive to the house and both women could clearly see a motor car turn in at the gate and stop at the front door. It was obviously a hired car, as the driver was not in livery, but the tall, mulled-up figure in unfamiliar clothes who occupied the front seat was for the moment a mystery to them. Only Helen seemed to have some wonderful premonition of the truth, a premonition which she was afraid to admit even to herself. Her hand began to shake. Philippa looked at her in amazement.

"You look as though you had seen a ghost, Helen!" she exclaimed. "Who on earth can it be, coming at this time of the day?"

Helen was speechless, and Philippa divined at once the cause of her agitation. She sprang to her feet.

"Helen, you don't imagine—" she gasped. "Listen!"

There was a voice in the hail—a familiar voice, though strained a little and hoarse; Mills' decorous greetings, agitated but fervent. And then—Major Richard Felstead!

"Dick!" Helen screamed, as she threw herself into his arms. "Oh, Dick! Dick!"

It was an incoherent, breathless moment. Somehow or other, Philippa found herself sharing her brother's embrace. Then the fire of questions and answers was presently interrupted by Mills, triumphantly bearing in a fresh dish of curry.

"What will the Major take to drink, your ladyship?" he asked.

Felstead laughed a little chokingly.

"Upon my word, there's something wonderfully sound about Mills!" he said. "It's a ghoulish thing to ask for in the middle of the day, isn't it, Philippa, but can I have some champagne?"

"You can have the whole cellarful," Philippa assured him joyously. "Be sure you bring the best, Mills."

"The Perrier Jonet 1904, your ladyship," was the murmured reply.

Mills' disappearance was very brief, and in a very few moments they found themselves seated once more at the table. They sat one on either side of him, watching his glass and his plate. By degrees their questions and his answers became more intelligible.

"When did you get here?" they wanted to know.

"I arrived in Harwich about daylight this morning," he told them; "came across from Holland. I hired a car and drove straight here."

"When did you know you were coming home?" Helen asked.

"Only two days ago," he replied. "I never was so surprised in my life. Even now I can't realise my good luck. I can't see what I've done. The last two months, in fact, seem to me to have been a dream. Jove!" he went on, as he drank his wine, "I never thought I should be such a pig as to care so much for eating and drinking!"

"And think what weeks of it you have before you?" Helen explained, clapping her hands. "Philippa and I will have a new interest in life—to make you fat."

He laughed.

"It won't be very difficult," he promised them. "I had several months of semi-starvation before the miracle happened. It was all just the chance of having had a pal up at Magdalen who's been serving in the German Army—Bertram Maderstrom was his name. You remember him, Philippa? He was a Swede in those days."

"What a dear he must have been to have remembered and to have been so faithful!" Philippa observed, looking away for a moment.

"He's a real good sort," Felstead declared enthusiastically, "although Heaven knows why he's turned German! He worked like a slave for me. I dare say he didn't find it so difficult to get me better quarters and a servant, and decent food, but when they told me that I was free—well, it nearly knocked me silly."

"The dear fellow!" Philippa murmured pensively.

"Do you remember him, either of you?" Felstead continued. "Rather good-looking he was, and a little shy, but quite a sportsman."

"I—seem to remember," Philippa admitted.

"The name sounds familiar," Helen echoed. "Do have some more chutney, Dick."

"Thanks! What a pig I am making of myself!" he observed cheerfully. "You girls will think I can't talk about any one but Maderstrom, but the whole business beats me so completely. Of course, we were great pals, in a way, but I never thought that I was the apple of his eye, or anything of that sort. How he got the influence, too, I can't imagine. And oh! I knew there was something else I was going to ask you girls," Felstead went on. "Have you ever had a letter, or rather a letter each, uncensored? Just a line or two? I think I mentioned Maderstrom which I should not have been allowed to do in the ordinary prison letters."

Felstead was helping himself to cheese, and he saw nothing of the quick glance which passed between the two women.

"Yes, we had them, Dick," Philippa told him. "It was one afternoon—it doesn't seem so very long ago. And oh, how thankful we were!"

Felstead nodded.

"He got them across all right, then. Tell me, did they come through Holland? What was the postmark?"

"The postmark," Philippa repeated, a little doubtfully. "You heard what Dick asked, Helen? The postmark?"

"I don't think there was one," Helen replied, glancing anxiously at Philippa.

Felstead set down his glass.

"No postmark? You mean no foreign postmark, I suppose? They were posted in England, eh?"

Philippa shook her head.

"They came to us, Dick," she said, "by hand."

Felstead was, without a doubt, astonished. He turned round in his chair towards Philippa.

"By hand?" he repeated. "Do you mean to say that they were actually brought here by hand?"

Perhaps something in his manner warned them. Philippa laughed as she bent over his chair.

"We will tell you how they came, presently," she declared, "but not until you have finished your lunch, drunk the last drop of that champagne, and had at least two glasses of the port that Mills has been decanting so carefully. After that we will see. Just now I have only one feeling, and I know that Helen has it, too. Nothing else matters except that we have you home again."

Felstead patted his sister on the cheek, drew her face down to his and kissed her.

"It's so wonderful to be at home!" he exclaimed apologetically. "But I must warn you that I am the rabidest person alive. I went out to the war with a certain amount of respect for the Germans. I have come back loathing them like vermin. I spent—but I won't go on."

Mills made his appearance with the decanter of port.

"I beg your ladyship's pardon," he said, as he filled Felstead's glass, "but Mr. Lessingham has arrived and is in the library, waiting to see you."

CHAPTER XXVIII

To Major Richard Felstead, Mills' announcement was without significance. For the first time he became conscious, however, of something which seemed almost like a secret understanding between his sister and his fiancée.

"Tell Mr. Lessingham I shall be with him in a minute or two, if he will kindly wait," Philippa instructed.

"Who is Mr. Lessingham?" Richard enquired, as soon as the door had closed behind Mills. "Seems a queer time to call."

Helen glanced at Philippa, whose lips framed a decided negative.

"Mr. Lessingham is a gentleman staying in the neighbourhood," the latter replied. "You will probably make his acquaintance before long. Incidentally, he saved Henry's life the other night."

"Sounds exciting," Richard observed. "What form of destruction was Henry courting?"

"There was a trawler shipwrecked in the storm," Philippa explained. "You can see it from all the front windows. Henry was on board, returning from one of his fishing excursions. They were trying to find Dumble's anchorage and were driven in on to that low ridge of rock. A rope broke, or something, they had no more rockets, and Mr. Lessingham swam out with the line."

"Sounds like a plucky chap," Richard admitted.

Philippa rose to her feet regretfully.

"I expect he has come to wish us good-by," she said. "I'll leave you with Helen, Dick. Don't let her overfeed you. And you know where the cigars are, Helen. Take Dick into the gun room afterwards. You'll have it all to yourselves and there is a fire there."

Philippa entered the library in a state of agitation for which she was glad to have some reasonable excuse. She held out both her hands to Lessingham.

"Dick is back—just arrived!" she exclaimed. "I can't tell you how happy we are, and how grateful!"

Lessingham raised her fingers to his lips.

"I am glad," he said simply. "Do you mean that he is in the house here, now?"

"He is in the dining room with Helen."

Lessingham for a moment was thoughtful.

"Don't you think," he suggested, "that it would be better to keep us apart?"

"I was wondering," she confessed.

"Have you told him about my bringing the letters?"

She shook her head.

"We nearly did. Then I stopped—I wasn't sure."

"You were wise," he said.

"Are you wise?" she asked him quickly.

"In coming back here?"

She nodded.

"Captain Griffiths knows everything," she reminded him. "He is simply furious because your arrest was interfered with. I really believe that he is dangerous."

Lessingham was unmoved.

"I had to come back," he said simply.

"Why did you go away so suddenly?"

"Well, I had to do that, too," he replied, "only the governing causes were very different. We will speak, if you do not mind, only of the cause which has brought me back. That I believe you know already."

Philippa was curiously afraid. She looked towards the door as though with some vague hope of escape. She realised that the necessity for decision had arrived.

"Philippa," he went on, "do you see what this is?"

He handed her two folded slips of paper. She started. At the top of one she recognised a small photograph of herself.

"What are they?" she asked. "What does it mean?"

"They are passports for America," he told her.

"For—for me?" she faltered.

"For you and me."

They slipped from her fingers. He picked them up from the carpet. Her face was hidden for a moment in her hands.

"I know so well how you are feeling," he said humbly. "I know how terrible a shock this must seem to you when it comes so near. You are so different from the other women who might do this thing. It is so much harder for you than for them."

She lifted her head. There was still something of the look of a scared child in her face.

"Don't imagine me better than I am," she begged. "I am not really different from any other woman, only it is the first time this sort of thing has ever come into my life."

"I know. You see," he went on, a little wistfully, "you have not taken me, as yet, very far into your confidence, Philippa. You know that I love you as a man loves only once. It sounds like an empty phrase to say it, but if you will give me your life to take care of, I shall only have one thought—to make you happy. Could I succeed? That is what you have to ask yourself. You are not happy now. Do you think that, if you stay on here, the future is likely to be any better for you?"

She shook her head drearily.

"I believe," she confessed, "that I have reached the very limit of my endurance."

He came a little nearer. His hands rested upon her shoulders very lightly, yet they seemed like some enveloping chain. More than ever in those few moments she realised the spiritual qualities of his face. His eyes were aglow. His voice, a little broken with emotion, was wonderfully tender. He looked at her as though she were some precious and sacred thing.

"I am rich," he said, "and there are few parts of the world where we could not live. We could find our way to the islands, like your great writer Stevenson in whom you delight so much; islands full of colour, and wonderful birds, and strange blue skies; islands where the peace of the tropics dulls memory, and time beats only in the heart. The world is a great place, Philippa, and there are corners where the sordid crime of this ghastly butchery has scarcely been heard of, where the horror and the taint of it are as though they never existed, where the sun and moon are still unashamed, and the grey monsters ride nowhere upon the sapphire seas."

"It sounds like a fairy tale," she murmured, with a half pathetic smile.

"Love always fashions life like a fairy tale," he replied.

She stood perfectly still.

"You must have my answer now, at this moment?" she asked at last.

"There are yet some hours," he told her. "I have a very powerful automobile here, and to-night there is a full moon. If we leave here at ten o'clock, we can catch the steamer to-morrow afternoon. Everything has been made very easy for me. And fortune, too, is with us—your vindictive commandant, Captain Griffiths, is in London. You see, you have the whole afternoon for thought. I want you only for your happiness. At ten o'clock I shall come here. If you are coming with me, you must be ready then. You understand?"

"I understand," she assented, under her breath. "And now," she went on, raising her eyes, "somehow I think that you are right. It would be better for you and Dick not to meet."

"I am sure of it," he agreed. "I shall come for my answer at ten o'clock. I wonder—"

He stood looking at her, his eyes hungry to find some sign in her face. There was so much kindness there, so much that might pass, even, for affection, and yet something which, behind it all, chilled his confidence. He left his sentence uncompleted and turned towards the door. Suddenly she called him back. She held up her finger. Her whole expression had changed. She was alarmed.

"Wait!" she begged. "I can hear Dick's voice. Wait till he has crossed the hail."

They both stood, for a moment, quite silent. Then they heard a little protesting cry from Helen, and a good-humoured laugh from Richard. The door was thrown open.

"You don't mind our coming through to the gun room, Phil?" her brother asked. "We're not—My God!"

There was a queer silence, broken by Helen, who stood on the threshold, the picture of distress.

"I tried to get him to go the other way, Philippa."

Richard took a quick step forward. His hands were outstretched.

"Bertram!" he exclaimed. "Is this a miracle? You here with my sister?"

Lessingham held out his hand. Suddenly Richard dropped his. His expression had become sterner.

"I don't understand," he said simply. "Somebody please explain."

CHAPTER XXIX

For a few brief seconds no one seemed inclined to take upon themselves the onus of speech. Richard's amazement seemed to increase upon reflection.

"Maderstrom!" he exclaimed. "Bertram! What in the name of all that's diabolical are you doing here?"

"I am just a derelict," Lessingham explained, with a faint smile. "Glad to see you, Richard. You are a day earlier than I expected."

"You knew that I was coming, then?" Richard demanded.

"Naturally," Lessingham replied. "I had the great pleasure of arranging for your release."

"Look here," Richard went on, "I'm groping about a bit. I don't understand. Forgive me if I run off the track. I'm not forgetting our friendship, Maderstrom, or what I owe to you since you came and found me at Wittenburg. But for all that, you have served in the German Army and are an enemy, and I want to know what you are doing here, in England, in my brother-in-law's house."

"No particular harm, Richard, I promise you," Lessingham replied mildly.

"You are here under a false name!"

"Hamar Lessingham, if you do not mind," the other assented. "I prefer my own name, but I do not fancy that the use of it would ensure me a very warm welcome over here just now. Besides," he added, with a glance at Philippa, "I have to consider the friends whose hospitality I have enjoyed."

In a shadowy sort of way the truth began to dawn upon Richard. His tone became grimmer and his manner more menacing.

"Maderstrom," he said, "we met last under different circumstances. I will admit that I cut a poor figure, but mine was at least an honourable imprisonment. I am not so sure that yours is an honourable freedom."

Philippa laid her hand upon her brother's arm.

"Dick, dear, do remember that they were starving you to death!" she begged.

"You would never have lived through it," Helen echoed.

"You are talking to Mr. Lessingham," Philippa protested, "as though he were an enemy, instead of the best friend you ever had in your life."

Richard waved them away.

"You must leave this to us," he insisted. "Maderstrom and I will be able to understand one another, at any rate. What are you doing in this house—in England? What is your mission here?"

"Whatever it may have been, it is accomplished," Lessingham said gravely. "At the present moment, my plans are to leave your country to-night."

"Accomplished?" Richard repeated. "What the devil do you mean? Accomplished? Are you playing the spy in this country?"

"You would probably consider my mission espionage," Lessingham admitted.

"And you have brought it to a successful conclusion?"

"I have."

Philippa threw her arms around her brother's neck. "Dick," she pleaded, "please listen. Mr. Lessingham has been here, in this district, ever since he landed in England. What possible harm could he do? We haven't a single secret to be learned. Everybody knows where our few guns are. Everybody knows where our soldiers are quartered. We haven't a harbour or any secret fortifications. We haven't any shipping information which it would be of the least use signalling anywhere. Mr. Lessingham has spent his time amongst trifles here. Take Helen away somewhere and forget that you have seen him in the house. Remember that he has saved Henry's life as well as yours."

"I invite no consideration upon that account," Lessingham declared. "All that I did for you in Germany, I did, or should have attempted to do, for my old friend. Your release was different. I am forced to admit that it was the price paid for my sojourn here. I will only ask you to remember that the bargain was made without your knowledge, and that you are in no way responsible for it."

"A price," Richard pronounced fiercely, "which I refuse to pay!"

Lessingham shrugged his shoulders.

"The alternative," he confessed, "is in your hands."

Richard moved towards the telephone.

"I am sorry, Maderstrom," he said, "but my duty is clear. Who is Commandant here, Philippa?"

Philippa stood between her brother and the telephone. There was a queer, angry patch of colour in her cheeks. Her eyes were on fire.

"Richard," she exclaimed, "you shall not do this from my house! I forbid you!"

"Do what?"

"Give information. Do you know what it would mean if they believed you?"

"Death," he answered. "Maderstrom knew the risk he ran when he came to this country under a false name."

"Perfectly," Lessingham admitted.

"But I won't have it!" Philippa protested. "He has become our friend. Day by day we have grown to like him better and better. He has saved your life, Dick. He has brought you back to us. Think what it is that you purpose!"

"It is what every soldier has to face," Richard declared.

"You men drive me crazy with your foolish ideas!" Philippa cried desperately. "The war is in your brains, I think. You would carry it from the battlefields into your daily life. Because two great countries are at war, is everything to go by—chivalry?—all the finer, sweeter feelings of life? If you two met on the battlefield, it would be different. Here in my drawing-room, I will not have this black demon of the war dragged in as an excuse for murder! Take Dick away, Helen!" she begged. "Mr. Lessingham is leaving to-night. I will pledge my word that until then he remains a harmless citizen."

"Women don't understand these things, Philippa—" Richard began.

"Thank heavens we understand them better than you men!" Philippa interrupted fiercely. "You have but one idea—to strike—the narrow idea of men that breeds warfare. I tell you that if ever universal peace comes, if ever the nations are taught the horror of this lust for blood, this criminal outrage against civilisation, it is the women who will become the teachers, because amongst your instincts the brutish ones of force are the first to leap to the surface at the slightest provocation. We women see further, we know more. I swear to you, Richard, that if you interfere I will never forgive you as long as I live!"

Richard stared at his sister in amazement. There seemed to be some new spirit born within her. Throughout all their days he had never known her so much in earnest, so passionately insistent. He looked from her to the man whom she sought to protect, and who answered, unasked, the thoughts that were in his mind.

"Whatever harm I may have been able to do," Lessingham announced, "is finished. I leave this place to-night, probably for ever. As for the Commandant," he went on with a faint smile, "he is already upon my track. There is nothing you can tell him about me which he does not know. It is just a matter of hours, the toss of a coin, whether I get away or not."

"They've found you out, then?" Richard exclaimed.

"Only a miracle saved me from arrest a week ago," Lessingham acknowledged. "Your Commandant here is at the present moment in London for the sole purpose of denouncing me."

"And yet you remain here, paying afternoon calls?" Richard observed incredulously. "I'm hanged if I can see through this!"

"You see," Lessingham explained gently. "I am a fatalist!"

It was Helen who finally led her lover from the room. He looked back from the door.

"Maderstrom," he said, "you know quite well how personally I feel towards you. I am grateful for what you have done for me, even though I am beginning to understand your motives. But as regards the other things we are both soldiers. I am going to talk to Helen for a time. I want to understand a little more than I do at present."

Lessingham nodded.

"Let me help you," he begged. "Here is the issue in plain words. All that I did for you at Wittenberg, I should have done in any case for the sake of our friendship. Your freedom would probably never have been granted to me but for my mission, although even that I might have tried to arrange. I brought your letters here, and I traded them with your sister and Miss Fairclough for the shelter of their hospitality and their guarantees. Now you know just where friendship ended and the other things began. Do what you believe to be your duty."

Richard followed Helen out, closing the door after him. Lessingham looked down into Philippa's face.

"You are more wonderful even than I thought," he continued softly. "You say so little and you live so near the truth. It is those of us who feel as you do—who understand—to whom this war is so terrible."

"I want to ask you one question before I send you away," she told him. "This journey to America?"

"It is a mission on behalf of Germany," he explained, "but it is, after all, an open one. I have friends—highly placed friends—in my own country, who in their hearts feel as I do about the war. It is through them that I am able to turn my back upon Europe. I have done my share of fighting," he went on sadly, "and the horror of it will never quite leave me. I think that no one has ever charged me with shirking my duty, and yet the sheer, black ugliness of this ghastly struggle, its criminal inutility, have got into my blood so that I think I would rather pass out of the world in some simple way than find myself back again in that debauch of blood. Is this cowardice, Philippa?"

She looked at him with shining eyes.

"There isn't any one in the world," she said, "who could call you a coward. Whatever I may decide, whatever I may feel towards you, that at least I know."

He kissed her fingers.

"At ten o'clock," he began—

"But listen," she interrupted. "Apart from anything which Dick might do, you are in terrible danger here, all the more if you really have accomplished something. Why not go now, at this moment? Why wait? These few hours may make all the difference."

He smiled.

"They may, indeed, make all the difference to my life," he answered. "That is for you."

He followed Mills, who had obeyed her summons, out of the room. Philippa moved to the window and watched him until he had disappeared. Then very slowly she left the room, walked up the stairs, made her way to her own little suite of apartments, and locked the door.

CHAPTER XXX

It was a happy, if a trifle hysterical little dinner party that evening at Mainsail Haul. Philippa was at times unusually silent, but Helen had expanded in the joy of her great happiness. Richard, shaved and with his hair cut, attired once more in the garb of civilisation, seemed a different person. Even in these few hours the lines about his mouth seemed less pronounced. They talked freely of Maderstrom.

"A regular 'Vanity Fair' problem," Richard declared, balancing his wine glass between his fingers, "a problem, too, which I can't say I have solved altogether yet. The only thing is that if he is really going to-night, I don't see why I shouldn't let the matter drift out of my mind."

"It is so much better," Helen agreed. "Try as hard as ever I can, I cannot picture his doing any harm to anybody. And as for any information he may have gained here, well, I think that we can safely let him take it back to Germany."

"He was always," Richard continued reminiscently, "a sort of cross between a dreamer, an idealist, and a sportsman. There was never anything of the practical man of affairs about him. He was scrupulously honourable, and almost a purist in his outlook upon life. I have met a great many Germans," Richard went on, "and I've killed a few, thank God!—but he is about as unlike the ordinary type as any one I ever met. The only pity is that he ever served his time with them."

Philippa had been listening attentively. She was more than ever silent after her brother's little appreciation of his friend. Richard glanced at her good-humouredly.

"You haven't killed the fatted calf for me in the shape of clothes, Philippa," he observed. "One would think that you were going on a journey."

She glanced down at her high-necked gown and avoided Helen's anxious eyes.

"I may go for a walk," she said, "and leave you two young people to talk secrets. I am rather fond of the garden these moonlight nights."

"When is Henry coming back?" her brother enquired.

Philippa's manner was quiet but ominous.

"I have no idea," she confessed. "He comes and goes as the whim seizes him, and I very seldom know where he is. One week it is whiting and another codling. Lately he seems to have shown some partiality for London life."

Richard's eyes were wide open now.

"You mean to say that he is still not doing anything?"

"Nothing whatever."

"But what excuse does he give—or rather I should say reason?" Richard persisted.

"He says that he is too old for a ship, and he won't work in an office," Philippa replied. "That is what he says. His point of view is so impossible that I can not even discuss it with him."

"It's the rummest go I ever came across," Richard remarked reminiscently. "I should have said that old Henry would have been up and at 'em at the Admiralty before the first gun was fired."

"On the contrary," Philippa rejoined, "he took advantage of the war to hire a Scotch moor at half-price, about a week after hostilities had commenced."

"It's a rum go," Richard repeated. "I can't fancy Henry as a skulker. Forgive me, Philippa," he added.

"You are entirely forgiven," she assured him drily.

"He comes of such a fine fighting stock," Richard mused. "I suppose his health is all right?"

"His health," Philippa declared, "is marvellous. I should think he is one of the strongest men I know."

Her brother patted her hand.

"You've been making rather a trouble of it, old girl," he said affectionately. "It's no good doing that, you know. You wait and let me have a talk with Henry."

"I think," she replied, "that nearly everything possible has already been said to him."

"Perhaps you've put his back up a bit," Richard suggested, "and he may really be on the lookout for something all the time."

"It has been a long search!" Philippa retorted, with quiet sarcasm. "Let us talk about something else."

They gossiped for a time over acquaintances and relations, made their plans for the week—Richard must report at the War Office at once.

Philippa grew more and more silent as the meal drew to a close. It was at Helen's initiative that they left Richard alone for a moment over his port. She kept her arm through her friend's as they crossed the hall into the drawing-room, and closed the door behind them. Philippa stood upon the hearth rug. Already her mouth had come together in a straight line. Her eyes met Helen's defiantly.

"I know exactly what you are going to say, Helen," she began, "and I warn you that it will be of no use."

Helen drew up a small chair and seated herself before the fire.

"Are you going away with Mr. Lessingham, Philippa?" she asked.

"I am," was the calm response. "I made up my mind this afternoon. We are leaving to-night."

Helen stretched out one foot to the blaze.

"Motoring?" she enquired.

"Naturally," Philippa replied. "You know there are no trains leaving here to-night."

"You'll have a cold ride," Helen remarked. "I should take your heavy fur coat."

Philippa stared at her companion.

"You don't seem much upset, Helen!"

"I think," Helen declared, looking up, "that nothing that has ever happened to me in my life has made me more unhappy, but I can see that you have reasoned it all out, and there is not a single argument I could use which you haven't already discounted. It is your life, Philippa, not mine."

"Since you are so philosophical," Philippa observed, "let me ask you—should you do what I am going to do, if you were in my place?"

"I should not," was the firm reply.

Philippa laughed heartily.

"Oh, I know what you are going to say!" Helen continued quickly. "You'll tell me, won't you, that I am not temperamental. I think in your heart you rather despise my absolute fidelity to Richard. You would call it cowlike, or something of that sort. There is a difference between us, Philippa, and that is why I am afraid to argue with you."

"What should you do," Philippa demanded, "if Richard failed you in some great thing?"

"I might suffer," Helen confessed, "but my love would be there all the same. Perhaps for that reason I should suffer the more, but I should never be able to see with those who judged him hardly."

"You think, then," Philippa persisted, "that I ought still to remain Henry's loving and affectionate wife, ready to take my place amongst the pastimes of his life—when he feels inclined, for instance, to wander from his dark lady-love to something petite and of my complexion, or when he settles down at home for a few days after a fortnight's sport on the sea and expects me to tell him the war news?"

"I don't think that I should do that," Helen admitted quietly, "but I am quite certain that I shouldn't run away with another man."

"Why not?"

"Because I should be punishing myself too much."

Philippa's eyes suddenly flashed.

"Helen," she said, "you are not such a fool as you try to make me think. Can't you see what is really at the back of it all in my mind? Can't you realise that, whatever the punishment it may bring, it will punish Henry more?"

"I see," Helen observed. "You are running away with Mr. Lessingham to annoy Henry?"

"Oh, he'll be more than annoyed!" Philippa laughed sardonically. "He has terrible ideas about the sanctity of things that belong to him. He'll be remarkably sheepish for some time to come. He may even feel a few little stabs. When I have time, I am going to write him a letter which he can keep for the rest of his life. It won't please him!"

"Where are you—and Mr. Lessingham going to live?" Helen enquired.

"In America, to start with. I've always longed to go to the States."

"What shall you do," Helen continued, "if you don't get out of the country safely?"

"Mr. Lessingham seems quite sure that we shall," Philippa replied, "and he seems a person of many expedients. Of course, if we didn't, I should go back to Cheshire. I should have gone back there, anyway, before now, if Mr. Lessingham hadn't come."

"Well, it all seems very simple," Helen admitted. "I think Mr. Lessingham is a perfectly delightful person, and I shouldn't wonder if you didn't now and then almost imagine that you were happy."

"You seem to be taking my going very coolly," Philippa remarked.

"I told you how I felt about it just now," Helen reminded her. "Your going is like a great black cloud that I have seen growing larger and larger, day by day. I think that, in his way, Dick will suffer just as much as Henry. We shall all be utterly miserable."

"Why don't you try and persuade me not to go, then?" Philippa demanded. "You sit there talking about it as though I were going on an ordinary country-house visit."

Helen raised her head, and Philippa saw that her eyes were filled with tears.

"Philippa dear," she said, "if I thought that all the tears that were ever shed, all the words that were ever dragged from one's heart, could have any real effect, I'd go on my knees to you now and implore you to give up this idea. But I think—you won't be angry with me, dear?—I think you would go just the same."

"You seem to think that I am obstinate," Philippa complained.

"You see, you are temperamental, dear," Helen reminded her. "You have a complex nature. I know very well that you need the daily love that Henry doesn't seem to have been willing to give you lately, and I couldn't stop your turning towards the sun, you know. Only—all the time there's that terrible anxiety—are you quite sure it is the sun?"

"You believe in Mr. Lessingham, don't you?" Philippa asked.

"I do indeed," Helen replied. "I am not quite sure, though, that I believe in you."

Philippa was a little startled.

"Well, I never!" she exclaimed. "Exactly what do you mean by that, Helen?"

"I am not quite sure," Helen continued, "that when the moment has really come, and your head is upturned and your arms outstretched, and your feet have left this world in which you are now, I am not quite sure that you will find all that you seek."

"You think he doesn't love me?"

"I am not convinced," Helen replied calmly, "that you love him."

"Why, you idiot," Philippa declared feverishly, "of course I love him! I think he is one of the sweetest, most lovable persons I ever knew, and as to his being a Swede, I shouldn't care whether he were a Fiji Islander or a Chinese."

Helen nodded sympathetically.

"I agree with you," she said, "but listen. You know that I haven't uttered a single word to dissuade you. Well, then, grant me just one thing. Before you start off this evening, tell Mr. Lessingham the truth, whatever it may be, the truth which you haven't told me. It very likely won't make any difference. Two people as nice as you and he, who are going to join their lives, generally do, I believe, find the things they seek. Still, tell him."

Philippa made no reply. Richard opened the door and lingered upon the threshold. Helen rose to her feet.

"I am coming, Dick," she called out cheerfully. "There's a gorgeous fire in the gun room, and two big easy-chairs, and we'll have just the time I have been looking forward to all day. You'll tell me things, won't you?"

She looked very sweet as she came towards him, her eyes raised to him, her face full of the one happiness. He passed his arm around her waist.

"I'll try, dear," he said. "You won't be lonely, Philippa?"

"I'll come and disturb you when I am," she promised.

The door closed. She stood gazing down into the fire, listening to their footsteps as they crossed the hall.

CHAPTER XXXI

Lessingham stood for a moment by the side of the car from which he had just descended, glanced at the huge tyres and the tins of petrol lashed on behind.

"Nothing more you want, chauffeur?" he asked.

"Nothing, sir," was the almost inaudible reply.

"You have the route map?"

"Yes, sir, and enough petrol for three hundred miles."

Lessingham turned away, pushed open the gate, and walked up the drive of Mainsail Haul. Decidedly it was the moment of his life. He was hard-pressed, as he knew, by others besides Griffiths. A few hours now was all the start he could reasonably expect. He was face to face with a very real and serious danger, which he could no longer ignore, and from which escape was all the time becoming more difficult. And yet all the emotionalism of this climax was centred elsewhere. It was from Philippa's lips that he would hear his real sentence; it was her answer which would fill him once more with the lust for life, or send him on in his rush through the night for safety, callous, almost indifferent as to its result.

He walked up the drive, curiously at his ease, in a state of suspended animation, which knew no hope and feared no disappointment. Just before he reached the front door, the postern gate in the wall on his left-hand side opened, and Philippa stood there, muffled up in her fur coat, framed in the faint and shadowy moonlight against the background of seabounded space. He moved eagerly towards her.

"I heard the car," she whispered. "Come and sit down for a moment. It isn't in the least cold, and the moon is just coming up over the sea. I came out," she went on, as he walked obediently by her side, "because the house somehow stifled me."

She led him to a seat. Below, the long waves were breaking through upon the rocks, throwing little fountains of spray into the air. The village which lay at their feet was silent and lifeless—there was, indeed, a curious absence of sound, except when the incoming waves broke upon the rocks and ground the pebbles together in their long, backward swish. Very soon the sleeping country, now wrapped in shadows, would take form and outline in the light of the rising moon; hedges would divide the square fields, the black woods would take shape and the hills their mystic solemnity. But those few minutes were minutes of suspense. Lessingham was to some extent conscious of their queer, allegorical significance.

"I have come," he reminded her quite steadily, "for my answer."

She showed him the small bag by her side upon the seat, and touched her cloak. She was indeed prepared for a journey.

"You see," she told him, "here I am."

His face was suddenly transformed. She was almost afraid of the effect of her words. She found herself struggling in his arms.

"Not yet," she begged. "Please remember where we are."

He released her reluctantly. A few yards away, they could hear the soft purring of the six-cylinder engine, inexorable reminder of the passing moments. He caught her by the hand.

"Come," he whispered passionately. "Every moment is precious."

She hesitated no longer. The open postern gate seemed to him suddenly to lead down the great thoroughfare of a new and splendid life. He was to be one of those favoured few to whom was given the divine prize. And then he stopped short, even while she walked willingly by his side. He knew so well the need for haste. The gentle murmur of that engine was inviting him all the while. Yet he knew there was one thing more which must be said.

"Philippa," he began, "you know what we are doing? We can escape, I believe. My flight is all wonderfully arranged. But there will be no coming back. It will be all over when our car passes over the hills there. You will not regret? You care enough even for this supreme sacrifice?"

"I shall never reproach you as long as I live," she promised. "I have made up my mind to come, and I am ready."

"But it is because you care?" he pleaded anxiously.

"It is because I care, for one reason."

"In the great way?" he persisted. "In the only way?"

She hesitated. He suddenly felt her hand grow colder in his. He saw her frame shiver beneath its weight of furs.

"Don't ask me quite that," she begged breathlessly. "Be content to know that I have counted the cost, and that I am willing to come."

He felt the chill of impending disaster. He closed the little gate through which they had been about to pass, and stood with his back to it. In that faint light which seemed to creep over the world before the moon itself was revealed, she seemed to him at that moment the fairest, the most desirable thing on earth. Her face was upturned towards his, half pathetic, half protesting against the revelation which he was forcing from her.

"Listen, Philippa," he said, "Miss Fairclough warned me of one thing. I put it on one side. It did not seem to be possible. Now I must ask you a question. You have some other motive, have you not, for choosing to come away with me? It is not only because you love me better than any one else in the world, as I do you, and therefore that we belong to one another and it is right and good that we should spend our lives in one another's company? There is something else, is there not, at the root of your determination? Some ally?"

It was a strange moment for Philippa. Nothing had altered within her, and yet a wonderful pity was glowing in her heart, tearing at her emotions, bringing a sob into her throat.

"You mean—Henry?" she faltered.

"I mean your husband," he assented.

She was suddenly passionately angry with herself. It seemed to her that the days of childishness were back. She was behaving like an imbecile whilst he played the great game.

"You see," he went on, his own voice a little unsteady, "this is one of those moments in both our lives when anything except the exact truth would mean shipwreck. You still love your husband?"

"I am such a fool!" she sobbed, clutching at his arm.

"You were willing to go away with me," he continued mercilessly, "partly because of the anger you felt towards him, and partly out of revenge, and just a little because you liked me. Is that not so?"

Her head pressed upon his arm. She nodded. It was just that convulsive movement of her head, with its wealth of wonderful hair and its plain black motoring hat, which dealt the death-blow to his hopes. She was just a child once more—and she trusted him.

"Very well, then," he said, "just let me think—for a moment."

She understood enough not to raise her head. Lessingham was gazing out through the chaotic shadows of the distant banks of clouds from which the moon was rising. Already the pain had begun, and yet with it was that queer sense of exaltation which comes with sacrifice.

"We have been very nearly foolish," he told her, with grave kindliness. "It is well, perhaps, that we were in time. Those windows which lead into your library,—through which I first came to you, by-the-by,—" he added, with a strange, reminiscent little sigh, "are they open?"

"Yes!" she whispered.

"Come, then," he invited. "Before I leave there is something I want to make clear to you."

They made their way rather like two conspirators along the little terraced walk. Philippa opened the window and closed it again behind them. The room was empty. Lessingham, watching her closely, almost groaned as he saw the wonderful relief in her face. She threw off the cloak, and he groaned again as he remembered how nearly it had been his task to remove it. In her plain travelling dress, she turned and looked at him very pathetically.

"You have, perhaps, a morning paper here?" he enquired.

"A newspaper? Why, yes, the Times," she answered, a little surprised.

He took it from the table towards which she pointed, and held it under the lamplight. Presently he called to her. His forefinger rested upon a certain column.

"Read this," he directed.

She read it out in a tone which passed from surprise to blank wonder:

Commander Sir Henry Cranston, Baronet, to receive the D.S.O. for special services, and to be promoted to the rank of Acting Rear-Admiral.

"What does it mean?" she asked feverishly. "Henry? A D.S.O. for Henry for special services?"

"It means," he told her, with a forced smile, "that your husband is, as you put it in your expressive language, a fraud."

CHAPTER XXXII

For a moment Philippa was unsteady upon her feet. Lessingham led her to a chair. From outside came the low, cautious hooting of the motor horn, calling to its dilatory passenger.

"I can not, of course, explain everything to you," he began, in a tone of unusual restraint, "but I do know that for the last two years your husband has been responsible to the Admiralty for most of the mine fields around your east coast. To begin with, his stay in Scotland was a sham. He was most of the time with the fleet and round the coasts. His fishing excursions from here have been of the same order, only more so. All the places of importance, from here to the mouth of the Thames, have been mined, or rather the approaches to them have been mined, under his instructions. My mission in this country, here at Dreymarsh—do not shrink from me if you can help it—was to obtain a copy of his mine protection scheme of a certain town on the east coast."

"Why should I shrink from you?" she murmured. "This is all too wonderful! What a little beast Henry must think me!" she added, with truly feminine and marvellously selfish irrelevance.

"You and Miss Fairclough," Lessingham went on, "have rather scoffed at my presence here on behalf of our Secret Service. It seemed to you both very ridiculous. Now you understand."

"It makes no difference," Philippa protested tearfully. "You always told us the truth."

"And I shall continue to do so," Lessingham assured her. "I am not a clever person at my work which is all new to me, but fortune favoured me the night your husband was shipwrecked. I succeeded in stealing from him, on board that wrecked trawler, the plan of the mine field which I was sent over to procure."

"Of course you had to do it if you could," Philippa sobbed. "I think it was very clever of you."

He smiled.

"There are others who might look at the matter differently," he said. "I am going to ask you a question which I know is unnecessary, but I must have your answer to take away with me. If you had known all the time that your husband, instead of being a skulker, as you thought him, was really doing splendid work for his country, you would not have listened to me for one moment, would you? You would not have let me grow to love you?"

She clutched his hands.

"You are the dearest man in the world," she exclaimed, her lips still quivering, "but, as you say, you know the answer. I was always in love with Henry. It was because I loved him that I was so furious. I liked you so much that it was mean of me ever to think of — of what so nearly happened."

"So nearly happened!" he repeated, with a sudden access of the bitterest self-pity.

Once more the low, warning hoot of the motor horn, this time a little more impatient, broke the silence. Philippa was filled with an unreasoning terror.

"You must go!" she implored. "You must go this minute! If they were to take you, I couldn't bear it. And that man Griffiths — he has sworn that if he can not get the Government authority, he will shoot you!"

"Griffiths has gone to London," he reminded her.

"Yes, but he may be back by this train," she cried, glancing at the clock, "and I have a strange sort of fancy — I have had it all day — that Henry might come, too. It is overdue now. Any one might arrive here. Oh, please, for my sake, hurry away!" she begged, the tears streaming from her eyes. "If anything should happen, I could never forgive myself. It is because you have been so dear, so true and honourable, that all this time has been wasted. If it were to cost you your life!"

She was seized by a fit of nervous anxiety which became almost a paroxysm. She buttoned his coat for him and almost dragged him to the door. And then she stopped for a moment to listen. Her eyes became distended. Her lips were parted. She shook as though with an ague.

"It is too late!" she faltered hysterically. "I can hear Henry's voice! Quick! Come to the window. You must get out that way and through the postern gate."

"Your husband will have seen the car," he protested. "And besides, there is your dressing-bag and your travelling coat."

"I shall tell him everything," she declared wildly. "Nothing matters except that you escape. Oh, hurry! I can hear Henry talking to Jimmy Dumble—for God's sake—"

The words died away upon her lips. The door had been opened and closed again immediately. There was the quick turn of the lock, sounding like the click of fate. Sir Henry, well inside the room, nodded to them both affably.

"Well, Philippa? You weren't expecting me, eh? Hullo, Lessingham! Not gone yet? Running it a trifle fine, aren't you?"

Lessingham glanced towards the fastened door.

"Perhaps," he admitted, "a trifle too fine."

Sir Henry was suddenly taken by storm. Philippa had thrown herself into his arms. Her fingers were locked around his neck. Her lips, her eyes, were pleading with him.

"Henry! Henry, you must forgive me! I never knew—I never dreamed what you were really doing. I shall never forgive myself, but you—you will be generous."

"That's all right, dear," he promised, stooping down to kiss her. "Partly my fault, of course. I had to humour those old ladies down at Whitehall who wanted me to pose as a particularly harmless idiot. You see," he went on, glancing towards Lessingham, "they were always afraid that my steps might be dogged by spies, if my position were generally known."

Philippa did not relinquish her attitude. She was still clinging to her husband. She refused to let him go.

"Henry," she begged, "oh, listen to me! I have so much to confess, so much of which I am ashamed! And yet, with it all, I want to entreat—to implore one great favour from you."

Sir Henry looked down into his wife's face.

"Is it one I can grant?" he asked gravely.

"If you want me ever to be happy again, you will," she sobbed. "For Helen's sake as well as mine, help Mr. Lessingham to escape."

Lessingham took a quick step forward. He had the air of one who has reached the limits of his endurance.

"You mean this kindly, Lady Cranston, I know," he said, "but I desire no intervention."

Sir Henry patted his wife's hand and held her a little away from him. There was a curious but unmistakable change in his deportment. His mouth had not altogether lost its humorous twist, but his jaw seemed more apparent, the light in his eyes was keener, and there was a ring of authority in his tone.

"Come," he said, "let us understand one another, Philippa, and you had better listen, too, Mr. Lessingham. I can promise you that your chances of escape will not be diminished by my taking up these few minutes of your time. Philippa," he went on, turning back to her, "you have always posed as being an exceedingly patriotic Englishwoman, yet it seems to me that you have made a bargain with this man, knowing full well that he was in the service of Germany, to give him shelter and hospitality here, access to my house and protection amongst your friends, in return for certain favours shown towards your brother."

Philippa was speechless. It was a view of the matter which she and Helen had striven so eagerly to avoid.

"But, Henry," she protested, "his stay here seemed so harmless. You yourself have laughed at the idea of espionage at Dreymarsh. There is nothing to discover. There is nothing going on here which the whole world might not know."

"That was never my plea," Lessingham intervened.

"Nor is it the truth," Sir Henry added sternly.

"The Baron Maderstrom was sent here, Philippa, to spy upon me, to gain access by any means to this house, to steal, if he could, certain plans and charts prepared by me."

Philippa began to tremble. She seemed bereft of words.

"He told me this," she faltered. "He told me not half an hour ago."

There was a tapping at the door. Sir Henry moved towards it but did not turn the key.

"Who is that?" he asked.

"Captain Griffiths is here with an escort, sir," Mills announced. "He has seized the motor car outside, and he begs to be allowed to come in."

CHAPTER XXXIII

Mills' words were plainly audible throughout the room. Philippa made eager signs to Lessingham, pointing to the French windows. Lessingham, however, shook his head.

"I prefer," he said gently, "to finish my conversation with your husband.'"

There was another and more insistent summons from outside. This time it was Captain Griffiths' raucous voice.

"Sir Henry Cranston," he called out, "I am here with authority. I beg to be admitted."

"Where is your escort?"

"In the hall."

"If I let you come in," Sir Henry continued, "will you come alone?"

"I should prefer it," was the eager reply. "I wish to make this business as little unpleasant to—to everybody as possible."

Sir Henry softly turned the key, opened the door, and admitted Griffiths. The man seemed to see no one else but Lessingham. He would have hastened at once towards him, but Sir Henry laid his hand upon his arm.

"You must kindly restrain your impatience for a few moments," he insisted. "This is a private conference. Your business with the Baron Maderstrom can be adjusted later."

"It is my duty," Griffiths proclaimed impatiently, "to arrest that man as a spy. I have authority, granted me this morning in London."

"Quite so," Sir Henry observed, "but we are in the midst of a very interesting little discussion which I intend to conclude. Your turn will come later, Captain Griffiths."

"I can countenance no discussion with such men as that," Griffiths declared scornfully. "I am here in the execution of my duty, and I resent any interference with it."

"No one wishes to interfere with you," Sir Henry assured him, "but until I say the word you will obey my orders."

"So far as I am concerned," Lessingham intervened, "I wish it to be understood that I offer no defence."

"You have no defence," Sir Henry reminded him suavely. "I gather that not only had you the effrontery to steal a chart from my pocket in the midst of a life struggle upon the trawler, but you have capped this exploit with a deliberate attempt to abduct my wife."

Griffiths seemed for a moment almost beside himself. His eyes glowed. His long fingers twitched. He kept edging a little nearer to Lessingham.

"Both charges," the latter confessed, looking Sir Henry in the eyes, "are true."

Then Philippa found herself. She saw the sudden flash in her husband's eyes, the grim fury in Griffiths' face. She stepped once more forward.

"Henry," she insisted, "you must listen to what I have to say."

"We have had enough words," Griffiths interposed savagely.

Sir Henry ignored the interruption.

"I am listening, Philippa," he said calmly.

"It was my intention an hour ago to leave this place with Mr. Lessingham to-night," she told him deliberately.

"The devil it was!" Sir Henry muttered.

"As for the reason, you know it," she continued, her tone full of courage. "I am willing to throw myself at your feet now, but all the same I was hardly treated. I was made the scapegoat of your stupid promise. You kept me in ignorance of things a wife should know. You even encouraged me to believe you a coward, when a single word from you would have changed everything. Therefore, I say that it is you who are responsible for what I nearly did, and what I should have done but for him—listen, Henry—but for him!"

"But for him," her husband repeated curiously.

"It was Mr. Lessingham," she declared, "who opened my eyes concerning you. It was he who refused to let me yield to that impulse of anger. Look at my coat there. My bag is on that table. I was ready to leave with him to-night. Before we went, he insisted on telling me everything about you. He could have escaped, and I was willing to go with him. Instead, he spent those precious minutes telling me the truth about you. That was the end."

"Lady Cranston omits to add," Lessingham put in, "that before I did so she told me frankly that her feelings for me were of warm friendliness—that her love was given to her husband, and her husband only."

"How long is this to go on?" Griffiths asked harshly. "I have the authority here and the power to take that man. These domestic explanations have nothing to do with the case."

"Excuse me," Sir Henry retorted, with quiet emphasis, "they have a great deal to do with it."

"I am Commandant of this place—" Griffiths commenced.

"And I possess an authority here which you had better not dispute," Sir Henry reminded him sternly.

There was a moment's tense silence. Griffiths set his teeth hard, but his hand wandered towards the back of his belt.

"I am now," Sir Henry continued, "going to announce to you a piece of news, over which we shall all be gloating when to-morrow morning's newspapers are issued, but which is not as yet generally known. During last night, a considerable squadron of German cruisers managed to cross the North Sea and found their way to a certain port of considerable importance to us."

Lessingham started, His face was drawn as though with pain. He had the air of one who shrinks from the news he is about to hear.

"Incidentally," Sir Henry continued, "three-quarters of the squadron also found their way to the bottom of the sea, and the other quarter met our own squadron, lying in wait for their retreat, and will not return."

Lessingham swayed for a moment upon his feet. One could almost fancy that Sir Henry's tone was tinged with pity as he turned towards him.

"The chart of the mine field of which you possessed yourself," he said, "which it was the object of your visit here to secure, was a chart specially prepared for you. You see, our own Secret Service is not altogether asleep. Those very safe and inviting-looking channels for British and Allied traffic—I marked them very clearly, didn't I?—were where I'd laid my mines. The channels which your cruisers so carefully avoided were the only safe avenues. So you see why it is, Maderstrom, that I have no grudge against you."

Lessingham's face for a moment was the face of a stricken man. There was a look of dull horror in his eyes.

"Is this the truth?" he gasped.

"It is the truth," Sir Henry assured him gravely.

"Does this conclude the explanations?" Captain Griffiths demanded impatiently. "Your news is magnificent, Sir Henry. As regards this felon—"

Sir Henry held up his hand.

"Maderstrom's fate," he said, "is mine to deal with and not yours, Captain Griffiths."

Philippa was the first to grasp the intentions of the man who was standing only a few feet from her. She threw herself upon his arm and dragged down the revolver which he had raised. Sir Henry, with a shout of fury, was upon them at once. He took Griffiths by the throat and threw him upon the sofa. The revolver clattered harmlessly on to the carpet.

"His Majesty's Service has no use for madmen," he thundered. "You know that I possess superior authority here."

"That man shall not escape!" Griffiths shouted.

He struggled for his whistle. Sir Henry snatched it from him and picked up the revolver from the carpet.

"Look here, Griffiths," he remonstrated severely, "one single move in opposition to my wishes will cost you your career. Let there be no misunderstanding about it. That man will not be arrested by you to-night."

Griffiths staggered to his feet. He was half cowed, half furious.

"You take the responsibility for this, Sir Henry?" he demanded thickly. "The man is a proved traitor. If you assist him to escape, you are subject to penalties—"

Sir Henry threw open the door.

"Captain Griffiths," he interrupted, "I am not ignorant of my position in this matter. Believe me, your last chance of retaining your position here is to remember that you have had specific orders to yield to my authority in all matters. Kindly leave this room and take your soldiers back to their quarters."

Griffiths hesitated for a single moment. He had the appearance of a man half demented by a passion which could find no outlet. Then he left the room, without salute, without a glance to the right or to the left. Out in the hall, a moment later, they heard a harsh voice of command. The hall door was opened and closed behind the sound of retreating footsteps.

"Sir Henry," Lessingham reminded him, "I have not asked for your intervention."

"My dear fellow, you wouldn't," was the prompt reply. "As for the little trouble that has happened in the North Sea, don't take it too much to heart, it was entirely the fault of the people who sent you here."

"The fault of the people who sent me here," Lessingham repeated. "I scarcely understand."

"It's simple enough," Sir Henry continued. "You see, you are about as fit to be a spy as Philippa, my wife here, is to be a detective. You possess the one insuperable obstacle of having the instincts of a gentleman.—Come, come," he went on, "we have nothing more to say to one another. Open that window and take the narrow path down to the beach. Jimmy Dumble is waiting for you at the gate. He will row you out to a Dutch trawler which is lying even now off the point."

"You mean me to get away?" Lessingham exclaimed, bewildered.

"Believe me, it will cost nothing," Sir Henry assured him. "I was not bluffing when I told Captain Griffiths that I had supreme authority here. He knows perfectly well that I am within my rights in aiding your escape."

Philippa moved swiftly to where Lessingham was standing. She gave him her hands.

"Dear friend," she begged, "so wonderful a friend as you have been, don't refuse this last thing."

"Be a sensible fellow, Maderstrom," Sir Henry said. "Remember that you can't do yourself or your adopted country a ha'porth of good by playing the Quixote."

"Besides," Philippa continued, holding his hands tightly, "it is, after all, only an exchange. You have saved Henry's life, set Richard free, and brought us happiness. Why should you hesitate to accept your own liberty?"

Sir Henry threw open the window and looked towards a green light out at sea.

"There's your trawler," he pointed out, "and remember the tide will turn in half an hour. I don't wish to hurry you."

Lessingham raised Philippa's fingers to his lips.

"I shall think of you both always," he said simply. "You are very wonderful people."

He turned towards the window. Sir Henry took up the Homburg hat from the table by his side.

"Better take your hat," he suggested.

Lessingham paused, accepted it, and looked steadfastly at the donor.

"You knew from the first?" he asked.

"From the very first," Sir Henry assured him. "Don't look so confounded," he went on consolingly. "Remember that espionage is the only profession in which it is an honour to fail."

Philippa came a little shyly into her husband's arms, as he turned back into the room. The tenderness in his own face, however, and a little catch in his voice, broke down at once the wall of reserve which had grown up between them.

"My dear little woman!" he murmured. "My little sweetheart! You don't know how I've ached to explain everything to you—including the Russian ladies."

"Explain them at once, sir!" Philippa insisted, pretending to draw her face away for a moment.

"They were the wife and sister-in-law of the Russian Admiral, Draskieff, who was sent over to report upon our method of mine laying," he told her.

"You and I have to go up to a little dinner they are giving tomorrow or the next day."

"Oh, dear, what an idiot I was!" Philippa exclaimed ruefully. "I imagined—all sorts of things. But, Henry dear," she went on, "do you know that we have a great surprise for you—here in the house?"

"No surprise, dear," he assured her, shaking his head. "I knew the very hour that Richard left Wittenberg. And here he is, by Jove!"

Richard and Helen entered together. Philippa could not even wait for the conclusion of the hearty but exceedingly British greeting which passed between the two men.

"Listen to me, both of you!" she cried incoherently. "Helen, you especially! You never heard anything so wonderful in your life! They weren't fishing excursions at all. There weren't any whiting. Henry was laying mines all the time, and he's blown up half the German fleet! It's all in the Times this morning. He's got a D.S.O.—Henry has—and he's a Rear-Admiral! Oh, Helen, I want to cry!"

The two women wandered into a far corner of the room. Richard wrung his brother-in-law's hand.

"Philippa isn't exactly coherent," he remarked, "but it sounds all right."

"You see," Sir Henry explained, "I've been mine laying ever since the war started. I always had ideas of my own about mine fields, as you may remember. I started with Scotland, and then they moved me down here. The Admiralty thought they'd be mighty clever, and they insisted upon my keeping my job secret. It led to a little trouble with Philippa, but I think we are through with all that.—I suppose you know that those two young women have been engaged in a regular conspiracy, Dick?"

"I know a little," Richard replied gravely, "and I'm sure you will believe that I wouldn't have countenanced it for a moment if I'd had any idea what they were up to."

"I'm sure you wouldn't," Sir Henry agreed. "Anyway, it led to no harm."

"Maderstrom, then," Richard asked, with a sudden more complete apprehension of the affair, "was over here to spy upon you?"

"That's the ticket," Sir Henry assented.

Richard frowned.

"And he bribed Philippa and Helen with my liberty!"

"Don't you worry about that," his brother-in-law begged. "They must have known by instinct that a chap like Maderstrom couldn't do any harm."

"Where is he now?" Richard asked eagerly. "Helen insisted upon keeping me out of the way but we've heard all sorts of rumours. The Commandant has been up here after him, hasn't he?"

"Yes, and I sent him away with a flea in his ear! I don't like the fellow."

"And Maderstrom?"

"The pseudo-Mr. Lessingham, eh?" Sir Henry observed. "Well, to tell you the truth, Dick, if there is one person I am a little sorry for in the history of the last few weeks, it's Maderstrom."

"You, too?" Richard exclaimed. "Why, every one seems crazy about the fellow."

Sir Henry nodded.

"I remember him in your college days, Dick. He was a gentleman and a good sort, only unfortunately his mother was a German. He did his bit of soldiering with the Prussian Guards at the beginning of the war, got a knock and volunteered for the Secret Service. They sent him over here. The fellow must have no end of pluck, for, as I dare say you know, they let him down from the observation car of a Zeppelin. He finds his way here all right, makes his silly little bargain with our dear but gullible womenkind, and sets himself to watch—to watch me, mind. The whole affair is too ridiculously transparent. For a time he can't bring himself even to touch my papers here, although, as it happens, they wouldn't have done him the least bit of good. It was only the stress and excitement of the shipwreck last week that he ventured to steal the chart which I had so carefully prepared for him. I really think, if he hadn't done that, I should have had to slip it into his pocket or absolutely force it upon him somehow. He sends it off like a lamb and behold the result! We've crippled the German Navy for the rest of the war."

"It was a faked chart, then, of course?" Richard demanded breathlessly.

"And quite the cleverest I ever prepared," Sir Henry acknowledged. "I can assure you that it would have taken in Von Tirpitz himself, if he'd got hold of it."

"But where is Maderstrom now, sir?" Richard asked.

Sir Henry moved his head towards the window, where Philippa, for the last few moments, had softly taken her place. Her eyes were watching a green light bobbing up and down in the distance. Suddenly she gave a little exclamation.

"It's moving!" she cried. "He's off!"

"He's safe on a Dutch trawler," Sir Henry declared. "And I think," he added, moving towards the sideboard, "it's time you and I had a drink together, Dick."

They helped themselves to whisky and soda. There were still many explanations to be given. Half-concealed by the curtain, Philippa stood with her eyes turned seawards. The green light was dimmer now, and the low, black outline of the trawler crept slowly over the glittering track of moonlight. She gave a little start as it came into sight. There was a sob in her throat, tears burning in her eyes. Her fingers clutched the curtains almost passionately. She stood there watching until her eyes ached. Then she felt an arm around her waist and her husband's whisper in her ear.

"I haven't let you wander too far, have I, Phil?"

She turned quickly towards him, eager for the comfort of his extended arms. Her face was buried in his shoulder.

"You know," she murmured.